Rance
Rainey:
The Christmas Kid

~~~

By,
Jim Wade Smith

Jim Wade Smith

~ ~ ~

Cover Design & Editing:
Lara Martin

Cover Photo provided royalty free via:
pixabay.com
Photographs of Jim Wade Smith by Lara Martin

~ ~ ~

Meadow Creek Books
Copyright © 1980-2016 Jim Wade Smith

ISBN: 0692731261
ISBN-13: 978-0692731260

I dedicate this book to Matthew, my grandson, who borrowed my deer rifle, walked into the woods behind my house, and shot his first whitetail buck. He was 15 at the time.

~~~

CONTENTS

~~~

1
~ <u>AT THE SCHOOL</u> ~

*H*e was a real sorry man. About as sorry as they come, was old man Periwinkle. *'He had no cause, no cause a 'tall, whipping Jori Lee that way just because her ma had turned him down.'*

Jori Lee's Ma was widowed, and old man Periwinkle had tried to take advantage of the fact. But Elizabeth Jane Rainey was having none of it. I sat here in the dust beside the schoolhouse and I grinned. *'Old Periwinkle had sure bit off more than he could chew that time! Libby had put the rollers under the varmint with that cap and ball colt of Bill Rainey's. He stepped mighty high and handsome when the forty four ball's dusted his toes! It almost made me laugh right out loud just thinking about it.'*

Libby was my adopted ma, and I was some proud of her. She was a lady, and I loved her. If Bill had been alive, old Periwinkle wouldn't have dared to come sneaking around, grinning an' winkin' at my ma. I wanted to whip him then and there, but Libby forbad me to do it.

"Just as soon as we get back on our feet, you'll be wantin' to go back to school, son, and it won't do for you ta' be at odds with the teacher," she said.

"I don't care," I gritted through clenched teeth. "I won't

3

go back to school. You need me too much on the ranch now that Pa's gone, so I'm gonna whip him!"

I was some mad at the schoolmaster, and I never liked him anyhow. I always had a bad temper, and sometimes something hot and fiery would come over me and I'd just kind of go crazy mad for a while. Bill Rainey had seen it in me and he'd look at me kind of funny, like he was real worried about me, and then he set me down by the crick an' talked to me real serious like.

"Son, ya' gotta' learn ta' master that temper a' your'n. If you don't, I'm afraid that someday it'll cause you a lot of trouble. You got ta' master it, or else, it'll master you. Anything that you can't master is your master!

"Rance," he said real gentle-like, "I love you just like you were my own son. You been a good boy, and I'm proud o' you. I want you to promise me that you'll try to control that temper a'fore you kill somebody, or maybe get killed. It would break Libby's heart, if something like that was to happen. And I guess it would just about kill Jori Lee. She loves you, Rance, and not like a brother, either. I've seen it in her and I'm some pleased. I reckon I approve, but I'm not asking you how you feel . I'll let you make up your own mind about Jori Lee, but I reckon I know your mind already and I'm not worried about it.

Old Bill was real good to me, and I loved him, so he didn't have to ask me twice. I promised him then and there, that I'd master the dark rages that laid hold on me and I'd make all of them proud of me. I meant it, too. I reckon he told Libby about it because when I started out ta thrash the ground with old Periwinkle, she looked at me like I was a snake in the grass, and she said,

"Reckon you're forgettin' your promise!" Well that just about took the wind out of all my sails, and I felt the hot sting of tears in my eyes. I couldn't cry, I just couldn't cry, because it was weakness in a man, and I was the man of the house now. I swallowed just as hard as I could, and the lump in my throat went away.

"Now, don't you worry any about ol' Periwinkle," Libby smiled at me and said, "I reckon I kin handle his kind any day o' the week an' then some!" Then she got out that old gun of Pa's and dusted the school master's britches so close ah gnat couldn't have flew between the bullets and the seat of his pants.

I still wished I could have whipped him but I guess it was worth it to see him run that way, all gawky, an awkward, like a crane out of water!

Pa taught me to shoot with that old cap and ball, and I got real good with it, too. Bill, er, I mean Pa, I still get mixed up sometimes on what to call him, made me practice all the time. Anytime, that is, that we could afford powder and lead. And in the end, he'd looked at me kind ah' respectful-like and he said,

"I Reckon you're better with ah' hand gun now than I ever was."

That was all he said, but that was saying an all-fired lot! Old Bill was some shakes with a gun, folks swore to it. He won all the shooting matches around this part of the country, and the people living around about cut their teeth on guns. The country was still an all fired long way from being civilized, what with rustlers and such. But old' Bill was gone now!

I was feeling tears in my eyes again, and I had to blink them away fast. Ma was still wearing black, *ah' 'mournin' him.'* Just ten days ago old Bill had been alive. I don't know why folks called Pa, *'Old Bill Rainey'.* He hadn't even reached forty years old, but folks still called him old Bill

Rainey.

'I guess it was because he had a way of looking out of them black eyes of his that made you know that here was a man who had been over the mountain. He was a good man to ride the river with, as the sayin' goes.

"Boy, you figure out what is right and honest and honorable, an' then you stand up for it so you'll never be ashamed to look a man in the eye!" Bill taught me all that he knew, and I loved him, just like he was my own pa.

Ten days ago he had been alive, but now he was dead. He was breaking in a new bronc' and the cinch strap broke. It just wasn't fair, for a man as good as Pa to be killed by a sorry, rotten, cinch strap! It wasn't fair at all! Pa's saddle was old, and money was hard to come by in the Texas brush country. There was nothing but wild steers and cactus and heat that would fry a lizard before you could spit!

Pa always repaired most everything when it broke, but I guess that he waited just one day too long to fix that old saddle strap, or maybe we was all out of cured leather. Anyway, you looked at it, Pa was gone and it was up to me to protect Ma and Jori Lee.

I had gone to school until Pa died, and just as soon as we were able to afford a hired man to help out Ma said that I would be going back to school to catch up on my education. Old Bill and Libby set a lot of store by education, and reading books and such. Not that I didn't like books or anything. I'd read *"Ivanhoe"* and parts of the Bible, too. Most of them, *'scriptures,'* as Pa called them made a lot of sense when you thought about it. All except for the "begets." I never could make sense out of those. I couldn't pronounce the names; they looked about a mile long to me. It'd read about like this: "Old so-and-so begat, Ishmael, and Ishmael begat, what's-his-name, and what's-his-name begat, who-was-it, and who-was-it begat, whatcha-call-him. It just seemed to me like there was just a whole lot of be-gattin' going on, which was some confusin' too!

I liked books though. They told about people and places far away, and adventures that I liked to pretend that I was taking part in along with the people that were doing them. It seems to me that people who don't read books are missing out on a lot of fun in life. I guess that I kind of liked going to school, too. All except for that ornery, good for nothing, school master!

Easing myself up closer to the window of the one room schoolhouse, I watched old Periwinkle. I had my reasons for spyin', which I won't go into at the moment. Mr. Oliver P. Periwinkle was a tall scarecrow of a man, given more to an undertaker's looks than a schoolmaster, to my way of thinking. Old Bones, the kids called him when they could be sure that he wasn't around. They were all afraid of him.

Well, he'd been the first, but he wouldn't be the last to try to sweet talk Libby Rainey. She was a mighty handsome woman, most as tall as a man, with long blonde hair and eyes as blue as an October morning sky. Jori Lee had taken after her only by having her blue eyes. The rest of Jori's good looks came from Bill Rainey. She had long black hair, all glossy and shiny. It had a scent that smelled fresh and wonderful. Her hair was kind of wavy-like. There was one curl that was always dropping down over her left eye and she was always tossing her head and blowing it out of her way. Her skin was dark and brown as an injun, and her teeth were white and perfect. She favored old Bill in looks but I figure it sure didn't hurt her a bit. She was just about the prettiest sixteen year old in Texas, bar none!

I hitched myself up and peeked in the window again. Like I said before, I was spying on Old Bones and if what I'd heard was true, there was going to be trouble. Maybe even whipping trouble!

Old Bones was just starting the spelling bee. So far nothing bad happened, but you never could tell, he'd be getting around to Jori any minute now. If what Johnny Hansen said was true and old Bones was whipping Jori Lee unmercifully there was gonna be a come upepence! I felt a little guilty when I looked at Jori Lee. She wouldn't like it if she knew what I was thinking and planning to do. But women folk just don't understand, sometimes. I had thought some on what pa had told me and I decided that I was in the right.

"No man lets his women folk be mistreated, not if he's a man! Stand up for what is right," Pa had said to me, so you won't be ashamed. I knew that if I didn't stand up to Old Bones, and protect Jori Lee, and my ma I would be ashamed for the rest of my life.

"You've got to have sand, boy," Pa told me once, and I guess I did have sand, too! Oh, I was afraid, sometimes, like the time that me and that bully Rusty Harris got into a fight. He was always picking on the little kids and making them cry. He'd pull the girls hair and throw their books in the mud and stuff like that.

Rusty was the biggest boy in school and I was afraid of him. The day he pulled Jori's hair and hit little Johnny Hansen in the head with a rock, cutting his scalp, causing it to bleed, I just couldn't stand it anymore.. So, even though I knew that I was afraid of him, I heard myself tell Rusty that I was gonna' whip him.

"Oh, yeah?" He said and then he pushed Jori Lee down in the mud. My temper had taken about as much as it could stand and I just kind of went crazy. I heard a scream that was half-growl, which must have been me because Rusty turned kind of white and scared looking just before I lit' in on him. I'd been afraid of him but I whipped him! Both of his eyes were blackened and his nose was bleeding. His face was scratched up something awful. I guess it did a little good though, because Rusty was real nice to the other kids after that.

When I got home Pa was waiting for me.

"Boy, Jori Lee told me that you've been fighting," Pa said to me and I said,

"Yes sir, I have."

"Did you whip him fair and square?" Pa asked me and I said yes but that I had been afraid at first. I had guessed that fact made me a coward. Pa looked at me straight,

"Son, a man thet ain't afraid of anything is a dang fool! That's not bravery, it's just plain foolishness. A brave man is one thet's afraid and knows he might get hurt, but he goes on and does what he has to do anyways. Don't you ever forget it!"

I guess I just didn't like Rusty pushing Jori Lee. She teased me unmerciful sometimes, just like a little sister, but we weren't blood kin. Somehow, I had never called her my sister, and she didn't call me brother, either. I guess we both knew that it went a lot deeper than that.

There were other times that she would grow quiet and mysterious-like, just staring at me with those big, deep blue eyes. They were as dark as that deep pool of water in the crick, where the big old trout liked to hide. No, she wasn't my sister, I was an orphan.

My folks had been unknown travelers in a single wagon just looking for a place to rest and call home. They found it together in the hot Texas sun, with Comanche arrows flying and scalping knives flashing blood red. He made a stand, had my pa, but it was pitifully little against the Comanche. He killed two and my ma got one with a butcher knife before they cut her down. I didn't remember much about my folks, I was too little at the time, but old Bill told me what had happened from the sign. When my ma saw the injuns, she sat me down on the side of the wagon away from them and told me to run and hide in the brush. At least, that's what old Bill figured she did.

Quick as a wink, I did just what my ma told me. The Comanche didn't see me, mainly because the wagon was between me and them. I crawled under a fallen tree where the brush was thick and the leaves covered me completely. I thought that I was playing hide and seek, so I hid myself real good.

'Pa'll give them old injuns what for,' I thought proudly. To a little boy, which I was at the time, a few dozen Comanche were nothing compared to my Pa. But my Pa and Ma had fallen dead before my eyes, while the Indians whooped fiendishly and raised their bloody scalps high into the air.

I saw, and heard, and in terror I covered up my eyes, and ears with my hands, whimpering like a little wounded animal. Those injuns didn't find me, though. From the wagon to where I was hid was solid rock so they couldn't track me. Ma's quick thinking saved my life!

Two days later, old Bill Rainey found me next to the barn wall, crying and shivering. He took me into Libby and she comforted me as best as she could. I cried, but I wouldn't talk. Libby cried too.

"Poor little feller, he's seen something terrible happen. Just look at all that blood. It's not his blood, for he is not hurt nowhere that I can find. It must be his folk's blood. They might be needin' help real bad!"

Bill Rainey quickly saddled his horse and back tracked me to the wagon. It was burned, and the bodies of a young man and woman lay side by side in the sun. After the injuns had left, I had come out of my hiding spot and went to my Ma and Pa, that's where I got all bloody. I kissed my mother and tried to get her and Pa to get up, but of course I was unsuccessful. After a while the need for water and food drove me away from the wagon.

"I'll come back as soon as I get somethin' to drink," I told them, but I had gotten lost and wandered around until I ran into the barn in the dark. There, I had lain down to get out of the cold wind. That next morning, Bill found me. He kept me and named me Rance after his grandpa, Rance Rainey, who fought in the War for Independence.

When I look in the mirror, I see a boy anywhere from sixteen to seventeen years old. Six feet tall in my stocking feet and my shoulders were nearly as wide as Bill Rainey's. My skin is well tanned, and I have jet black eyes that catch fire when I get mad. There wasn't any information about my folks to tell who I was or for that matter, who they had been. Bill and Libby guessed at my age, and I told everybody that my birthday was on Christmas.

I did a man's work and Jori Lee did a woman's work. There was plenty of work to go around. It was just a small spread, me an old Bill ran it without any hired hands. There were just a few cows and a few horses that old Bill broke himself.

I was torn out of my daydreaming by the raw sound of a hickory stick striking flesh. Rage, and sick disgust boiled up in me as I looked in the open window of the school house.

"That's the third word this week that you have misspelled, Jori Rainey, and you'll get the same thing now as you got then, Missy!"

Oliver P. Periwinkle was a picture of sadistic wrath, red-faced and breathing in hard, gasping grunts. Jori stood before him silent, tears coursing down her cheeks. This angered the school master even more and he drew back the stick to strike again. I jumped in the open window, and was shaking, I was so mad.

"No, you don't Mr.!" I yelled at the top of my voice and it must have scared old Bones because he staggered backwards, and fear made the white of his eyes roll and glisten. He took another step backwards.

"I'm gonna whip you….I'm gonna whip you just like you been whippin' Jori Lee!" I was some mad at that sorry, no account school teacher! Old Bones noticed then that it wasn't a grown up that was confronting him but only me, the orphan boy that belonged to Libby Rainey.

His mouth opened two or three times, and then he gritted his teeth together until they popped, he was so mad. He stepped toward me, brandishing the hickory stick in his hand.

"Get out of here, boy or I'll give you a taste of what your sister got!" I eyed Old Bones real mean like.

"I told you mister, I'm gonna whip you!" Advancing on the schoolmaster, I wasn't caring if he hit me or not.

"I'll stand no interference from the likes of you!" Periwinkle shouted as he jumped forward, hitting me across the shoulders with his hickory stick. It smarted some, but all it done was make me even more mad than before. I just smiled at Old Bones and kept advancing towards him. He hit me in the face, then, and I tasted blood from my busted lips and teeth. Right about then is when I turned from boy into a man! Periwinkle screamed,

"I'll teach you… you cur! I'll teach all of you Rainey's! Turn me down, will she? Well, I told her she'd be sorry! I'll make you all sorry!"

He swung that hickory stick again and again as I kept advancing towards him. He hit me more times than I could count, but then he finally backed up against the wall and couldn't back up any more! I smashed him against the wall and the peeled logs of that old schoolhouse shook all the way to the ground. All of the girls were screaming, and the boys cheered,

"Get em', Rance," I heard them say, "Whip him good! He's been whippin' Jori Lee for anything and everything. Hit him, Rance!"

And I did hit him! My knuckles cracked against the cadaverous face of old Bones! He lost the hickory stick as he went down, rolled over and tried to run on his hands and knees, scuttling for the door.

Right then I knew he was yellow and he just couldn't take it when the going got hot! But I wasn't willing to let him off that easy. He'd hurt me with that hickory, my teeth were loose and my face was swelling, turning blue. So I dove on him as he had taken out for the door. He gouged at my eyes more than once as we rolled over and over. Grunting, and kicking, we over turned the wood box, knocking down the stove pipe, scattering kindling wood all over the floor.

Soot was flying all over the place. Some of it got in my eyes. I knuckled them, trying to see better but that just caused the soot to sting my eyeballs. Old Bones grabbed a sizeable stick of that kindling wood and laid me up beside the head just as I got up on my feet! Lights burst in my head and I staggered falling to one knee. I was dazed, hearing him scream in triumph when he pulled that long, yellow handled knife from his boot.

"Now, I'll cut you, you young whelp!"Jori Lee screamed

as she threw herself on the schoolmaster.   She scratched his face with both hands before he backhanded her to the floor. As he turned back to face me, I moved fast and grabbed his knife arm with both hands.

Now, I got big hands and arms and they are some strong too! So I clamped down on Old Bone's wrist with one hand and I grabbed his elbow with the other, bending his arm backwards. He flailed at me with the other arm, gouging at my eyes with his fingers, but I just tightened my grip, gritted my teeth and laid on the pressure!

I lifted our wagon once when a wheel had come off so Pa could fix it. I held it off the ground until he put the wheel back on. When he got the wheel on, Pa turned around to me and grinned, and I grinned right back. He didn't have to say anything, I knew he hadn't believed that I could do it, but I did and he was pleased. There were two bags of feed in the wagon, too! They weighed a hundred pounds apiece!

Old Bones screamed when his arm busted! That long knife fell to the floor, the schoolmaster, moaning, held his broken arm. I then done a fool thing, I turned my back on a man who was my enemy. It was a mistake. I reckoned that the fight was over, but Periwinkle didn't. When I turned my back to leave, he grabbed his knife again with his left and lunged at me with it. The kid's screams warned me and I sidestepped, getting my body out of the way of that knife, but not my left arm. The knife sliced through the cloth of my sleeve, gashing my arm. I threw a hard, wicked right to the schoolmaster's jaw! It sent him backwards, staggering, and tripping over the kindling on the floor. His feet went every which way, crashing head first into the cast iron stove! The sound of his head hitting, real solid-like was loud and he lay still where he landed.

Standing there, with my legs spread and my fist clenched, I was breathing pretty hard, my head and face was bloody.

"Yeay," cheered the boys. "That was some fight! You whipped him good Rance, Old Bones got just what he deserved!" They were grinning from ear to ear. Jori put her arms around my neck and I didn't mind it at all, no sir!

"Ohhh, Rance," she sobbed brokenly, "I'm so sorry, I'm so sorry! It was all my fault!"

"Don't be sorry Jori Lee," I said, "It wasn't your fault, it was his! He's a poor excuse fer ah man! Johnny told me what was going on, he told me how Old Bones whipped you every chance he got, and how he was taking his spite for your ma, out on you. There ain't nobody gonna hurt you, Jori Lee, not as long as I'm alive!"

She smiled real pretty and touched where I hurt. I felt like I was ten feet tall!

"Rance!" Johnny Hanson's voice was choked with fear. "He's dead! Old Bones is dead! He busted his head on the stove!"

Suddenly I didn't feel so tall. I felt sick, sick to my stomach! At Johnny's words there was a shocked silence, and then pandemonium broke loose as the kids raced for the door. There was a struggle to see who would go through the door first, finally the bodies untangled and burst from the schoolhouse. One and all ran down the road screaming,

"He's dead, Old Bones is dead! Rance Rainey killed him! Rance Rainey killed the schoolmaster! They all disappeared down the road, still screaming. Jori Lee pulled at my arm desperately.

"Rance, c'mon, we gotta run! We gotta get home ta Ma! She'll know what to do, hurry Rance!"

"Wait for me!" Johnny Hansen cried out. "Wait for me! All the way home I kept thinking, *'I killed a man! I killed a man and they hang you for it!'* I'd seen a hangin' once and I didn't want to see another one. Some folks got a morbid curiosity to see death and blood, but not me! I seen all that I wanted to see when my Ma and Pa got killed by the Comanche! No, I didn't want to see a hangin'. Especially if it was my own! And what was Ma gonna say? I'd broken my promise to Pa! I'd lost my temper and now I had killed a man. That was just what Pa had said would happen if I didn't learn to control my temper!

2
~ <u>THE SHERIFFS KIN</u> ~

*S*omething deep inside of me kept telling me that it had been self-defence, and that if I hadn't done something about Old Periwinkle mistreating Jori Lee, something worse could have happened. That something worse was Elizabeth Jane Rainey.

I had me a bad feeling. A feeling that told me that Elizabeth Rainey wouldn't have liked what Old Bones had been doing to Jori, either! That bad feeling was this, Libby couldn't have whipped the schoolmaster, but she would have done the only thing that she could have to stop him! She would have shot the rascal, since she was woman enough to do it, too! She'd killed injuns and varmints before, when she and Bill first started the ranch.

The country was wilder then and folks learned to defend what they had. There was no law, which was bad, I guess, but there's always been something worse than no law and order. That is when the law is crooked! Everybody knows to defend themselves in a lawless land. By the time folks find out that the law is crooked, it's generally too late to help them selves. Pa told me once,

"Judge a man for him self and trust no man, even if he

wears a badge. It's best to not trust any man with your life or your loved one's lives. Look out for yourself and always hedge your bets, son." I found out that Bill Rainey was right most every time. The law around our part of the country was crooked, and most everybody knew it by now.

Sheriff Dexter was a low-down, back-shootin', crooked sneak of a man! He would be coming for me, soon I figured, real soon! There was one thing that made me sure that he'd be coming, ol' Sheriff Dexter was Oliver P. Periwinkle's half-brother! I shore had me a bear by the tail this time, and I didn't know how to turn it loose, either!

Sheriff Dexter didn't scare me half as much as having to face Ma, though! The closer we got to the house, the more I dreaded it.

"What would it do to her?" I wondered. "Pa said it would break her heart. If that happened, I guess that I couldn't stand it, because I loved her so much. As soon as we got to where we could see the house, we could see her standing underneath the big, old, cottonwood where Pa was buried. She'd go out there and stand, just lookin' at the grave and sometimes she'd cry.

Ma wasn't one to let anything get her down, though! She was a fighter. Elizabeth Jane Rainey was her full name and what she wanted she usually got. The day that she had laid eyes on Bill Rainey she decided that she wanted him. It made no matter to her that folks said that Bill was an outlaw. They said that Bill Rainey had killed a man who had murdered his Pa. Rumor had it that Bill had ridden the Owl Hoot Trail, and that he knew most all of the bad men who traveled that trail. Bill's Pa had been shot down in cold blood, without even a chance to defend himself. People said that it was over a woman, but Bill himself had never mentioned the matter to me. He was a quiet man most of the time, and I couldn't ever remember when he had broken a promise to me or anyone else.

Pa Rainey, which is what I called him sometimes, always kept his word. I never saw the day or the time when he refused a stranger or friend a nights lodging or a meal. I remember one time when two strangers had ridden up to the ranch house on horses that looked like they had come far and fast. Their horses were about done in. They were covered with dust and sweat. The men riding them didn't look to much better, either.

"Hello," Bill said to the tall slim one.

"How's the family," the man replied. "I heard that you were doing right well, and glad I am to hear it."

"The family's fine, Libby and I've added one more since you was by here last." Bill pointed to me. "Light and set boys," he said, "and we'll talk over old times together."

"We can't stay long," said the tall, slim one again, we're travelling light and kind of in a hurry."

"I understand, boys. Come on in, the boy will take care of your horses. Rub them down, son," he said to me, "and then give them a double handful of grain. Water em first, though, and when you get done, lead these fellers horses around back of the house and tie 'em with a slip knot to the back porch where they'll be out of the sun."

I led those horses down to the creek and watered them. Then I rubbed them down like Pa asked. When I got the dust and sweat off of them, I could see that these horses weren't just your ordinary run-of-the-mill cow pony. They were long legged, deep chested, built for speed and endurance. When I got done feeding them, I tied them up like Pa had told me to the porch in back of the house. I washed up for supper and walked around to the front porch where Pa and those two fellers were sittin'. They was talking low and somehow I knew it just wasn't the time to go butting into things, so I just stood back studying the ground and the way the ants run every which way, crazy-like. I then sauntered over to the big cottonwood, intending to study the horse's tracks, but there wasn't any! Someone had brushed em' away! Pa taught me to notice things, especially tracks and such. I could study a track and put it way back in my mind, if I ever ran into that particular track again, I'd know it. Those men stayed for supper and left when the moon rose full and yellow.

"Pa Rainey, who was those two men?" I asked him.

"Never mind, son, just you never mind," he answered me gently, and then he walked down to the creek, standing with his arms crossed behind him. I could see the butt of that big, old, colt pistol a' stickin' up out of his holster. He wore that gun all of the time. When he took it off, which was seldom, it was always within arm's reach. He stood there by the creek for a long time, just looking at the water, listening to the music it made. I watched him for a while until I got sleepy, then I went in and went to bed. I heard him come in after a long time, I then fell asleep.

A couple of days later, some of the boys at school said that Ben Thompson and Texas Jack had been seen riding around our part of Texas. I didn't say anything because I loved Old Bill Rainey and I knew that he wouldn't do anything to be ashamed of. If he'd killed a man, it was stand up, and face to face! Elizabeth Jane must have thought so too, for she walked right up to Bill the very same day that she saw him for the first time, and she said,

"Mr., they say that you are an outlaw and a bad man, but I like you, and I think they are wrong. I think you're a good man. If you are a mind to, you may call on me."

Bill Rainey did call on her. They were married a couple

of months later, Bill had escaped the rope, and a posse's bullets. Sometimes, even if a man's honorable, society condemns him, because he meets violence with violence. He defends those he loves with his life. Most people believe that fear of the law is sufficient to prevent wrong-doing, but Pa always said,

"Son, remember this, every man has the God given right to protect his life, and those of his loved ones. Any law that goes against a man protecting what's his, is a dishonorable law! Punishing a bad man does not excuse the law for failing to protect his victims! Protection is mostly in your hands, remember that. You must fight to live, but fight honorably, face to face, and do it fair and square." That was the day that he started teaching me how to use a gun.

"Remember son," he told me, "The law punishes wrong, but the prevention of wrong you hold in your hand, your gun! You must know how to use it. The life of someone you love could very well depend upon it!" Those words stuck in my mind, and I practiced with a thought to them. Old Bill taught me everything that he knew, and it was enough. Up to now, that is. I was in trouble with the law, and the law was crooked!

"Ma's over by the cottonwood." Jori Lee, said miserably.

"Call her over here, I can't tell her what I've got to tell her, while she's grievin' for Pa and standin' by his grave!"

"Self defense, that's what it was!" Libby snorted. My Ma was mad. I was afraid that she'd be mad at me but she wasn't. She was mad at ol' Periwinkle!

"Good riddance, I say!" She stomped around every which way.

"It's all my fault!" Jori Lee's big blue eyes filled and

overflowed with tears. "If I hadn't misspelled that word, this never would have happened!"

"Bosh! Now you listen to me, young lady, it's not your fault so don't you go blamin' yourself! Periwinkle was mad at me, and he was whipping you because of it. What Rance did was right. He defended you when you were being mistreated, and I'm proud of him. It's just what my Bill would have done! Libby looked at the grave under the cottonwood, and then she went on.

"Trouble is, Periwinkle is half brother to that low down ninny of a sheriff! Dexter's crooked as a lightnin's streak! I don't trust him to do right by you, Rance. You'll have to hide someplace safe where Dexter can't find ya until we can see what's going to happen and if you're gonna get a fair trial. It wouldn't do for you to take off now anyway, you wouldn't have enough lead on a possy. You'll just have to wait until after dark. Besides, you might not have to go. Just let Jori Lee know where to find you so we can get back together and decide what the best thing to do is."

Me and Jori lee looked at each other, and fear for me made her eyes real big and round.

"Our place!" I grinned at her, and then I ran toward the creek. Just after dark Jori Lee came for me. She slipped down to where a waterfall was; she dove into its pool and came up behind the wall of water where there was a small cave. It wasn't a big cave, just a small hollowed out place in the rock, maybe eight or nine feet back. We had found it one day when we were swimming and kept it a secret between us by writing our names on the wall and calling it our place, though I doubt if it had been unknown to Pa. he knew about everything almost before it happened.

"Rance!" Her voice sounded half fearful, as if she expected me to be gone.

"I'm here, Jori Lee." I whispered. She crawled over beside me and I took her into my arms and held her as tight as I could. Her face was wet, and I tasted the salt of her tears when I kissed her.

"Ohh, Rance" she sobbed, "He came…the sheriff came, and he said that they was gonna hang you! He had two men with him, real mean-lookin' men! I was afraid of them. The slim, shifty-eyed one kept staring at me an' grinning. His name was Jason and the other one, the big black-bearded one was called Buck. They're kin to Dexter, too! Dexter wanted to search the house but Ma told him to keep his dirty carcass out of her nice, clean house. She held daddy's big old gun on Dexter and she told him that she would shoot him if he tried to search the house!" Jori Lee Paused for breath, and then, she went on.

"Ma told him that Periwinkle pulled a knife on you and that it was a case of self defense. But old Dexter swore that there wasn't a knife found and that you killed Oliver with a stick of wood! Ohhh, they are framing you, Rance! The sheriff told Ma that what the kids say doesn't count in court, because they are too young to testify. He said that minors ain't allowed to testify, anyways! Ohhh, Rance you'll have to run! Jori Lee broke down and cried. I put my arms around her again and comforted her.

"Oh, I'll be alright, Jori Lee, your dad taught me a heap, and someday I'll be back and I'll marry you."

"Oh Rance, really.. You'll marry me?" She smiled through her tears and she kissed me. She said real fierce-like,

"I reckon I love you, Rance Rainey, so just remember that I claim you for my man, and there'll never be anybody else!"

"Sure honey," I told her, and there ain't nothing ever

gonna keep me away from you, Jori Lee!"

"C'mon," she whispered, "Ma's waitin'." We got to be careful too, the sheriff left the tall, thin one to watch the place. He's in the barn, asleep. Ma sent him down some pie and coffee. We put laudanum in it and he was drinking from a bottle of whiskey, too." Jori giggled, "He won't wake up for a week!"

Ma was waiting for us under the cottonwood with Pa's finest horse saddled. Its saddle bags full of the necessities I would need. She looked kind of small standing there beside Pa's grave.

"Son, you've got to ride far away. You can't come back until this thing clears away. I'm going to see to it that you're cleared, boy, no matter what happens." Her passionate, strong voice rose. "Come hell or high water!"

I felt a burning behind my eyes as I said goodbye to my home. Libby had been a good mother to me, and I noticed that she kept wiping her eyes with the back of her hand. Ma had sand, more than many a ma that I had seen. I hugged her to me and then after that Jori Lee kissed me so hard that it hurt. Ma shoved a ham biscuit into my hand as I mounted the horse, and said that there was more of it packed away. Quietly, I rode slowly away into the moonlight.

I had far to go before morning come. Men ain't supposed to cry but my face got wet after a while. I got mad, then. *If old Dexter came after me, he was gonna have big trouble on his hands. The world had given me some bad breaks, and I was through with rolling with the punches! From here on out, I'd throw a few of my own!* I stopped and looked back for one last look, then I took a look around for the North Star, when I saw it, I kicked my horse north.

3
~ THE OWL HOOT TRAIL ~

Come daylight, I was getting a little hungry, so I dug down into my saddlebags. The cold biscuits tasted real good and the side meat was plumb wonderful! It was getting time to hunt a place to lay up so I kept an eye out for a good place to rest. A man's got to sleep and so has his horse. The Appaloosa I rode was a prime saddle horse. Pa Rainey traded him off of some crow injuns once when he was up in Kansas on a trail drive. It took three horses and a Winchester to make the trade. That horse was Pa's pride and joy, next to his family, that was. Pa never had him gelded; he said that he was too good a horse to ruin that way.

Pa said that the Appaloosa was one of those Nez Perce' horses and that there wasn't any better in the world. Those crows probably stole the stallion from the Nez Perce'. They were great horse thieves, the crows, and they were proud of it too. That appaloosa stallion hadn't been broke in spirit, and he was real cantankerous and mean. He'd bite, or kick and he could buck like a keg of powder going off. He was old Bill's horse and nobody else could do a thing with him. He tolerated me, but that was about all. Him, and Pa's old

Navy Colt was about all I had in the world now, except Pa's fifty caliber sharps. I could beat Pa with a handgun, but I never saw anybody beat old Bill with a rifle. It just couldn't be done. I came close, though. But, that old needle gun just seemed to be a part of Pa Rainey. It seemed like no matter which way he pointed it, he always hit dead center. He shot it with what seemed like no effort at all.

I rode north a while, then I cut west for the Llano Estacado. I had me two full canteens and a water skin. If Dexter and his two hard cases followed me, they were in for a hard ride. Pretty soon, the sun was bearing down real hot and I took a drink from the water skin. There wasn't much water to be found in these parts. You had to know where to look. I kept an eye out for sinks and catch basins, where run off from the rain collected.

It didn't rain too often in this country, and when it did, the dry-cracked earth soaked it up faster'n ah drunk drinkin' whiskey on a Saturday night. I had me a drink of whiskey once! One of those men that sometimes stopped at the ranch slipped it to me. It burned my tongue and scorched my insides like a forest fire in July.

When Pa heard me choking and trying to get my breath, he knew what had happened. He watched me with his eyes hard as nails, and then he hit the fellow that gave me the bottle. That man went down like he was pole-axed, and he didn't come to until Pa threw water on him.

"Git on yer animal and dust the trail mister,"Pa growled, with his hand on his gun. That man was mad. He wanted to kill Pa, but he didn't draw. He got on his horse and he rode away from there. That was the first time and the only time that I got a tanning from old Bill.

"Son, liquor an' bad women have killed many ah man. As long as you kin' stay away from both of them!" And so far I had because I worshipped Old Bill Rainey.

After a while, I turned and I watched my back trail from the shade of a big old boulder. There wasn't any sign of anything or anyone following me but I knew that if the sheriff caught up with me, I'd never make it back to town for a trial. He'd claim that I'd tried to escape. Old Periwinkle's relatives were about as sorry as he was. The whole bunch was sorrier than watered down gravy!

"I wonder how Ma and Jori Lee was making it?" I was some worried about them. I felt guilty for running off and leaving them. After a while I stopped and made camp on a high rocky promontory over looking my back trail. I rubbed the Appaloosa down and nearly got kicked doing it.

Then I heated up some coffee in an old can that I carried for the purpose. When the coffee was boiling, I poured myself a cup of the black, mean lookin' stuff. It scalded my tongue, but it tasted good. I sat there watching my back trail, sippin' coffee and eating some more of Ma's cold biscuits. When I was through I put out the fire real good and I buried the ashes. I had to sleep some before I rode on, and the stallion could use some rest, just in case I had to run for it later. I wanted him fresh and ready to go, just in case I had me a run-in with ol Dexter and his pards!

I woke up a while later, still sleepy, but knowing that it was time to be movin' on. I tightened the cinch on my saddle, swung up and headed down the trail real cautious-like. That ornery stallion took it into his mind to be mean, and he put his head down and threw up his heels, squeelin' and buckin'. It made me mad, clear through and I was about to teach that horse a lesson in manners when the bullet hit! It smacked into a boulder right where my head had been a moment before!

I kicked the stallion into a run out of there! We went off

down the trail, threading through the rocks and brush, jumping the little ones and dodging the big ones. I heard the whine of more lead passing close, but I didn't feel anything. Pretty soon the trail began to rise again through a jumble of rocks and sand.

I pulled up behind a big cedar and tied the Appaloosa, and then I ran to my back trail where it started up the hill. They were just getting close to the bottom of the hill when that big old Sharps fifty caliber of my Pa's went off. Naturally I aimed at old Dexter. His hat went off his head like it was a bird, and he squalled like a baby. They whirled around a clump of cedar, and then holed up in some rocks. From the shadows of the rocks, I could see where they left their horses, and crawled up behind some boulders. I had them and they knew it. There just wasn't any way for them to get out of there without getting shot up.I had the elevation, and a better field of fire.

"Give up, boy," Dexter hollered, and his voice echoed around in the rocks spooky-like. "Ya can't git away from me an' my men! We's all skilled trackers an' ya cain't beat three a'gin one, so ya just, better give up!

I laid up there and grinned. Somebody was bluffin' and it sure wasn't me. I saw one of their legs move and I snapped off a shot, taking the heel and most of the man's spur from his boot. There was a wild yell. And the foot was jerked back out of sight.

"Go on home Dexter," I yelled, "before I get mad!"

"Yore under arrest fer murder, boy, now jest come on down here real peacefull-like and I'll see thet you git ah' fair trial!"

For my answer, I put a shot into the rock Dexter was hiding behind, shattering lead every which way. Then thinking of those shadows on the rocks I pulled me a bead about where those fellow's horses were.

I couldn't see them but I could see their shadows, and that let me know just about where they were standing. Now I didn't want to kill the horses, but I had to stop those men somehow. There was a big rock face next to where I figured those hosses were, so I bounced one of those big three hundred red grain bullets off it. There wasn't nothing happened, so I shifted my aim a little higher and I cut drive again. The resulting squeal from one of their hosses made them sit up and take notice.

"He's shootin' at tha' horses!" I heard one of Dexter's men cuss. I then cut loose again. A ricochet leaves a mighty bad wound. When I shot, them hosses just went wild. They bucked and squealed broke loose and stampeded back down the trail, leaving old Dexter and those men a foot!

I could have left then, but I didn't. I was still mad. They had fired on me without giving me a chance. They would have killed me too but for the stallion buck-jumping back yonder. So, I jest started bouncing bullets off the rocks around them. There was another yell and then I heard old Dexter holler.

"Don't shoot no more, boy, we give up! We'll all die down here from them ricochets!"

"Hell, I aint givin' up!" yelled one of them sorry hardcases. "You're yaller Dexter! Ya can't even handle a wet nosed kid! Well, I can handle em' and I will!" Then he came out of the rocks shootin' wild. I let him shoot and when his guns were empty, I aimed real careful an bounced another bullet around in the rocks where he took cover! I heard him yell out when the lead hit him!

"Ohhhh you good fer nuthin' kid, you've torn my arm off! Help, Buck, Dexter, I'm gonna bleed to death!" I listened to him beg for help but neither Dexter nor the other man moved, they was afraid to.

"Dexter," I yelled, come out of those rocks with your hands up. Throw your guns where I can see them, now, because I won't be givin' yun's another chance!"

"Ok, ok boy, we're ah' comin', don't shoot!" Dexter stepped out real careful with his hands up.

"Walk over to that open place there, Dexter! You with the beard, drag your pard over there with you." I watched the big man as he half dragged the wounded man over to the open.

"Ok, Kid, now what?" I looked at them close. I wanted to know them if I ever ran into them men again.

"Now see here, boy," Dexter blustered. "Ya can't do this!"

"Take em off!" I gritted, feeling mean. "Quick!"

"OK, OK," Dexter whined. The man with the beard glared at me with yellow hate filled eyes.

"You just remember, boy, you're gonna see me again, real soon."

"I hope not," I told him. "I hate to see a man throw away his chance at a living! If I ever see you again, I'll kill you! Now step back away from those clothes!" I went through their clothes and found a derringer in the bearded man's boot. And a long yellow handled knife in Dexter's filthy britches.

"You didn't find a knife, huh! Whatcha call this?" Dexter glared, but he made no answer. I held up the knife, it was the same one Periwinkle pulled on me. The initials 'OP' were carved into the handle. I pocketed the knife and the derringer. I then took their weapons. The wounded man groaned in pain. The ricochet had caught his left arm at the shoulder, ripping sideways, across the muscle, tearing a ragged and bloody gash.

"You'd better bandage his arm," I told blackbeard, "or else he'll bleed to death!"

I had taken their ammunition as well, and walked away. Then I turned and said,

"Don't come after me, for I'll kill every one of you if you do!" I walked to my Appaloosa and rode off due north where there was a trading post. When I got there, I traded their guns for more grub and shells. I then moved on quickly as I got there.

Two days later, I walked the stallion into a one store, one saloon town. There was a lot of places like this one. You could find them at places where trails crossed and where men from the ranches close around could come, drink and spend their thirty ah' month. I tied the stallion outside the saloon and pushed aside the blanket that was hung in place of the door.

The building was a slap-dash, ramshackle affair thrown together as if by accident. I stood outside for a minute and closed my eyes before I entered. When I went in my eyes were already adjusting themselves to the dark, dim interior of the place. Two men stood at the rough plank that served for a bar. Whisky barrels supported it on each end and a few fly-speckled glasses and bottles were perched on a shelf behind the bar keep.

I kept my hand close to my gun as I walked over and sat down on a packing crate that served as a chair, two more crates were stacked in front to serve as the table. I shifted the crate to put my back to the wall.

"What'll it be, mister?" The barkeep asked grudgingly.

"Grub!" I looked him square in the eyes as I said it. He spoke a little more politely then.

"Got some pretty good steaks, but they're antelope and a little tough on the jaw. You still interested?"

"I'm still interested," I answered.

"Comin' right up!" He walked to the back of the building and yelled at the Mexican cook.

"Hey Pancho, fry me up some steak and potatoes, will ya, an' be quick about it!" He then walked back around the bar. He was fat and bald with a handlebar mustache. What little hair he had was grayish brown.

I sat there with my hand close to the butt of my gun and watched the two men at the bar. Both of em wore beat up hats and chaps. They looked just like two ordinary cow punchers until I noticed their guns. They were tied down low and they looked well cared for. Now a cowhand uses his guns for everything from killin' rabbits to nailing staples into fence posts. Those men's guns weren't beat up at all. The butt's of the weapons were well polished from use, but they were well cared for. They were gunmen! They probably never punched a cow except to steal it, I decided. Those two would bear watchin', so I watched!

After a while they began to get uncomfortable with me sitting there just watching them.

"Ya see something that ya don't like, kid?" One of em placed his glass on the bar.

"Just thinkin'," I replied kind of dumb-like.

"Thinkin' what, mister?" the man growled and turned towards me.

"Thinkin' how much that steak's gonna cost me, for I'm nigh broke, and I hate ta wash dishes." He stared at me and then he grinned.

"Harry, here charges an arm and a leg fer one o' them pieces of leather he calls steaks, and it'll either be raw or burned to ah fare-the-well when ya get it! Pancho can't cook for little apples." Harry glared at the man,

"What're you tryin' to do, Mac, run my trade off? Mac

32

guffawed and slapped his leg, and then he tossed the last of his drink down.

"C'mon Bob, let's go!" Pancho appeared, carrying the steak and potatoes, which he set in front of me. After the two men went out, I started to eat. Like Mac had said, the steak was burned and the potatoes were half-raw. I chewed the tough steak, while I sawed at what was left. Even so, it tasted good for I was mighty hungry. Then I saw the blanket pull back, Mac and Bob reentered, bellying up to the bar and ordering drinks again!

I hadn't missed the furtive, sneaky looks that had passed between them. They were after something, but what? I kept eating, and watching the two buzzards. Then they sauntered over to stand in front of me.

"I just seen yore hoss, kid, an' I'm wonderin' where ya got an animal like that?" Mac's voice was hard. Before I could answer, because my mouth was full, he made his claim.

"I'm claimin' that hoss o' yorn and I'm callin' you a low-down hoss thief! What ya got ta say about that?" He grinned, and winked at his partner. Bob didn't grin; he just stood there with his eyes kind of vacant. I swallowed the piece of steak and answered, real quiet and gentle-like.

"It could be. Pa traded him off of some red skins. When did you lose him?" Well that set him back some. Most people would have gone off half-cocked and started to argue the point. Mac had been all set and primed for gunplay, but now it looked to him as if he was getting the horse for nothing.

"About a year ago." He said, winking again at Bob. Bob never moved. He was dangerous, I decided, by far the more dangerous of the two. He was tall and thin, with long arms and an undershot jaw.

He kept his eyes on my right hand, just waiting for me to go for my gun. His hand hovered over his gun butt. I had a fork in my gun hand and I'd never make it to my gun! I was good, but I knew that no man's that good.

"Well," I drawled out, "better luck next time boys, my pappy's had that hoss nigh onto three years now! I got ah bill of ownership too, registered with the county. Sorry."

"It don't matter," Mac said with a snicker. "We was gonna take him anyhow!"

"You were wrong about the steaks, Mac" I said good-naturedly.

"Huh?" he said, looking at me as if I was crazy.

"This is mighty fine steak." I said, spearing another piece. I jammed the fork against the plate, causing it to skid and fly out of my hand to the right. Their eyes followed the fork for an instant, just long enough to give me an even break. Bob's gun was coming up as I thumbed Pa's old Navy colt twice, then a third time for Mac! The barkeep had his hands on the shot gun before I saw him. It went off into the ground when my forty-four slug caught him in the throat! He gurgled and fell across the plank bar, over turning it and spilling whiskey and glasses.

Blood and whisky mixed and seeped into the sawdust on the floor. Turning, I covered the back.

"Come out of there, Pancho, and now! I ordered.

"S-s-Si Senor, I come, I come queek!" Pancho had his hands so high in the air he was standing on tip toe. I said,

"Pancho, this here is now your place. The former owner has passed away leaving it to you. He made an oral will, and I will personally stand as a witness to the matter. Do you not agree? I smiled. Pancho's eyes lit up with realization of what I had just said.

"Oh, si senor, si! He leave saloon to Pancho, gracias,

senor!"

"Now, I said, "All personal effects of deceased will go to pay for my meal and your broken merchandise. I believe that I will have another steak, cooked more carefully this time, Si?"

"Si!" Grinned Pancho, then he took his arms down and disappeared into the back again. I examined the bodies, keeping the rear entrance in plain sight. The two holes in Bob had taken the center from the bull durham tag hanging from his left, front pocket. Mac's took the button from the same pocket. That barkeep, now that was a bad shot, course taking into account of I was kind of in a hurry, it wasn't too bad. I'd have to practice a little though, a man had to keep his hand in.

Some people might think that I should have tried to talk those men out of trying to kill me, and I'm sure that some would say that I shouldn't have shot them. But these men had the advantage, and their kind just doesn't show mercy to their victims. Pa had taught me the way of survival and it was a hard lesson. These men had intended to kill me for my horse and my guns. I felt no remorse for defending myself. I was just glad to be alive. Pa always said,

"Son, a bullet don't care who it kills, and that's final. If you don't look out for yourself you won't last long in this country.

I dragged the bodies outside then I went back in and took my time eating my second steak. It was perfect. Pancho had out done himself. He was busy sweeping out the place, cleaning up the broken glass and blood stains. When I got up to leave he held up his hand.

"I give you grub, senor, you have made Pancho a reech man and he eees ever grateful." He fetched me a sack of grub. And grain for my horse.

"Eeef you need anythin' more, senor, Pancho ees proud to serve you. Barkeep, he own store too. He was one beeg horse thief. Those two bad men keel other men for their horses and guns. The barkeep sells the guns an' horses, and then they split the gold. You have made Pancho veer' reech! Gracias senor," He bowed, "mucho gracias!" I mounted the Appaloosa.

"What do you call this place, Pancho?"

"Whiskey, senor." I smiled.

"Whisky Town!" As I rode off, I looked back; Pancho was putting up a new sign. *Pancho's*, it read in big bold letters.

"Pancho's Whiskey Town!" I laughed.

4
~ <u>THE HERD</u> ~

*P*a's old Appaloosa was steppin' high and handsome. That horse shore liked to travel! I followed the back trails whenever I could, and seldom went into any of the settlements except when I had to have supplies. I was getting itchy lately, from riding and sleeping on the ground so much.

"Hoss," I said, "the first stream that we come to we're gonna get us a bath. Not a first rate one with a tub and all, but a bath just the same! That old spotted stallion laid his ears back and made a noise deep in his throat, then he reached around and tried to bite, showing his teeth.

"You ornery old devil, cut it out!"Then I grinned. "Devil," what was the Spanish word for devil…"Diablo?" Yeah, that was it! "Diablo!" Pa hadn't given that old horse a name, just called him the stallion. "Well, you got a name now you old crowbait, I mumbled. "From now on, your name's Diablo." That old horse shook his head and laid ears back. His mean eyes glinted wickedly.You never agree with anything, do you, you ornery, mean varmit?" I put him into a run and his ears came up. "There, you like that, don't you, you old devil! You like to run."We come to a stream and I pulled up so fast Diablo tried to bite again.

"Next time you try that I'm biting you back!" He must have believed me because all of a sudden, he settled down and let me take off the saddle and bridle. He only kicked at me once. I guess he was lookin' forward to that roll and bath, too. I jumped in that cold water with nothing on but my birthday suit. Pretty soon I was covered with chill bumps. It was cold, and my chill bumps had little chill bumps. Diablo rolled and kicked, then he came into the water just like he was gonna stomp me plumb down in the mud. He wallowed, and then he reached out to bite me again.

"I told you, you hard-headed mule, you!" I grabbed him around the neck. The water was deep, and I had him at a disadvantage. Before you could say, *'Scat'*, I had his ear in my mouth and I bit down hard. That old horse went haywire, but he couldn't stomp or kick for having to swim. I let him loose and he took out of the water just as fast as he came in. He shook himself just like a dog, and looked back over his shoulder at me as if to say, *'No fair, a man aint supposed to bite his hoss like that! It's supposed to be the other way around!'* I shook my fist at him.

"How do you like that, you old devil?" He pricked his ears at me and danged, if he didn't whicker at me like he used to whicker at Pa. He walked out into the grass and went to grazing.

I was putting on my clothes when I heard the bawling of cattle. I grabbed my hat and ran upstream to investigate. The sound of cattle got louder and I finally saw them crossing the stream about half a mile above me. I watched the drovers put the cattle into the water. Some of the cattle didn't want to go, and they'd charge the rider's horses. These were big old longhorns and they were wild and tough.

I sighed to myself. Pa had probably herded cattle up this very trail. I was about to turn to go back to gather up my gear when I heard the click of metal. It was a gun being cocked! Thinkin' on tryin' a dive sideways but a voice that was hoarse and raspy said,

"Don't try it, Pilgrim, I h'aint no tenderfoot, and I can't miss at this distance. In case yore wonderin', this hyar is ah fifty caliber sharps, and I got her set fine, real fine. Now, drop that gunbelt and walk on out in the open. I'll be right behind ya so, don't you try nothin' funny. In the Bible it says there's ah time fer everythin, ah time ta live and ah time ta die. This hyar is ah time to do like yore told, now git goin'!"

I believed him, so I did like he said. After we got out in the open, the fellah behind me hollered real loud.

"Hey, Big Ben Cole, I got me one o' them low down herd-cutters what's been followin' us. Come on, an' bring ah rope!"

He then hit me. My hands were tied behind my back and he hit me again. I tasted blood that came from my smashed lips and my nose was bleeding, too. I looked that man right back in the eye and I said,

"Mister, I done told ya, I ain't no herd cutter, but that don't matter none, now. You hit me when my hands was tied and I'm gonna kill you for it!" He knocked me down again. I felt the skin break over my left eye when the blow landed.

"Wheeccooooh!" One of the men whistled, "Ya shor hog tied you a curly wolf this time, Seth!" I raised myself to one knee and tried to get up. Seth kicked me back down with a knee in the face.

"That'll be about enough!" said the big red-headed man

who caught me.

"But he won't tell us where his pards are, Red, jest give me two more minutes with him an' I'll make him talk!"

"No!" Red thundered, "By Elijah ya won't, neither! I'd never brought him in if I'd knowed ye were gonna jump on him with both feet."

"We'll hang him then!" Seth cried venomously. One of the men threw a rope over a tree limb. A noose was already fashioned at the end. The red-haired man with the feather in his hat cocked his rifle,

"No, not that neither, not until the boss git's here!" The men didn't like it but they didn't have any choice but to wait. The man called Red looked like he meant what he said.

"What's goin' on here?" The biggest hunk of a man I ever saw in my life road up.

"Boss, Red caught him one of them herd-cutters that shot Seth's brother last week! We were just gettin' round ta stringin' him up, pronto!" Ike, the one who was siding with Seth was doing the talking. The big man looked at me and his eyes narrowed.

"Is that true, mister, are you one of those stinkin' herd-cutters?"

"No!" I said as loud as I could through my swelled up lips. "I don't know anything about any herd cutters. My horse is downstream with his saddle off and grazin'. I'm camped there and was watching you cross your herd when this man you call Red John jumped me!" It was some hard to talk with my busted mouth and all.

"That don't prove anything", Ike growled. "He could still be one of those skunks! I say hang him."

"Ike!" The big man said, "Shut yore mouth!" Ike backed up and sat down.

"Now boy," the big man drawled, "We got us some talkin' to do." He had a black beard, a handlebar mustache, and must have weighed three hundred pounds. He wasn't fat, though, not by a long shot!

"Cut him loose, Red!" he ordered.

"Shore boss, and glad to," answered Red. When my hands were free Red murmered to me,

"Sorry boy, I didn't know the skunks would hit a helpless man!" The minute my hands were free I made for Seth.

"Hold it, boy!" The one they called Big Ben held a forty four in his hand. "You gonna behave or do I have to tie ya again?"

"He hit me when I was tied!" I snapped through gritted teeth.

"Time enough for that, boy, you ain't off the hook yet!" Now what's your handle?"

"Rainey, Rance Rainey!" I didn't know if there were any hand bills out on me, so I answered him.

"And what are you doin' out here so far from the settlements?" Ben asked.

"Ridin'," I said.

"You gotta do better than that, son. Who are your folks and where are you from? I know it ain't the right thing to ask a man, but these are unusual circumstances. You might have killed one of my men. If you did we'll hang you!"

"My Pa was Bill Rainey, and I'm from down south of here!"

"Boss!" said one of the men, "the kid's lyin'! I knowed ol Bill Rainey, and he didn't have a boy!"

"He adopted me," I spoke up. Big Ben looked at me with doubt in his eyes.

"Son," he said real quiet. "You tell us as much as you

know about Old Bill Rainey, and you better make it good, because you'll hang if it doesn't ring true!"

"You there," I spoke to the man who'd said he knew my Pa. "You said you knew my Pa, how well did you know him?

"Well enough," came the answer.

"Bill Rainey married Elizabeth Jane Holcombe," I said, "and his daughter is called Jori Lee."

"Still don't prove anything." The man said.

"Bill was quiet, and quick with a gun," I replied, "and he knew some people that rode the high lonesome! He rode it himself for a while before he settled down."

"He had himself a hoss;" the man spoke up. "What color was it?"

"Mister," I said. "I'll show ya!" I looked at the Boss to get his ok to move towards my camp. He knodded and we all started downstream.

"I'm carryin' Pa's guns, too. A sharps fifty and his old forty four navy colt. His initials are on the butt, W.R.!" about that time we rounded the edge of the stream, all the cow punchers were anxiously waiting to see if what I had told them was the truth. We came into view of Pa's Appaloosa still grazing in the grass. The man looked the horse over. Then he saw that both my guns were clearly in view by my camp roll just as I had told them. He looked back at me queerly.

"He's who he says he is Boss!"

"Why, he could have stolen those things," Seth objected.

"Not off Old Bill, he couldn't," the stranger said. "There's not a man living who could do that unless old Bill was dead. I'm tellin' ya, this is ol' Bill Rainey's adopted son and I'm glad to shake your hand, boy!"

"Well, I'm right glad that I don't have ta hang ya, kid!' Big Ben stuck out his hand and I took it. I had me a hunch that Big Ben was straight stuff, and Red John, too, even if he did get me into this mess. He came sauntering up, rubbing his whiskers with one hand and saying sheepishly.

"Mister Rainey, I'm all fired sorry to have bothered ya, an' I'm beggin' yore pardon. Here's my hand, ya don't have to shake it if'n yore sore at me. I reckon I'd be some sore, too, an' I wouldn't blame ya none! Fer, tha record, my handle's Red John McDonald."

"I took his hand and pumped it. I'd have been buzzard bait, if you hadn't stood in, mister Red John, and I guess that squares things with me!"

"Here's your hog leg." Red said, and I took it. I checked the loads, and then buckled it around my waist.

"Seth, step up an' take your medicine!" My voice was loud. "I'm callin' you out an' you too, Ike! Let's see how you skunks can do against ah man that can defend himself!"

"Now hold on boy," Ben Cole spoke gruffly. "I know these men wronged you, but I need them to herd my cattle. Where in tarnation could I get men out here, I ask you?"

"I'll sign on!" I said shortly.

"I'm askin' you to let bygones, be bygones, son." Ben spread his hands.

"No!" I refused, "They beat me when I was helpless. Only a skunk would do a thing like that!"

"Then you'll have to take me on, too." Ben said.

"Wait a minute," The man who'd knew my Pa interrupted, "Boss, your makin' ah bad mistake! Son," he asked, "just how good are you with that gun?" I looked at the man.

"Pa Rainey taught me how to use it. He beat me at first,

but before I was done practicing, I was some better than him." I said. The man turned to Big Ben,

"Boss, I'd recommend you stay out of this affair! I understand how the boy feels and he's gonna do this no matter what. Besides, if he's anything like old Bill Rainey, he'd kill the three of you. Take my word for it."

"Well Seth, you comin' out or not?" I challenged. Seth stepped forward, but Ike was reluctant.

"Mr. I didn't hit you," he hedged.

"No," I answered him. "But you held me and tried your best to get me hung! Step up, Ike, it's payday for you!" He moved reluctantly up beside Seth.

"Seth! Your brother was killed, but I didn't have anything to do with it! I understand your feeling but that doesn't excuse you for hittin' me while my hands were tied. Fill your hand, mister!" I gritted.

"I ain't sorry I hit you," Seth snarled. "I ain't sorry a'tall, and now I'm gonna bore you full of holes!" He went for his gun, and then Pa's old navy colt bucked once in my hand just like it had been there all the time. Seth buckled, and fell forward on his face. Ike just stood there.

"I knew it!" The stranger said, "That kid is Old Bill Rainey all over again! Ike, you had better git on yore hoss and leave, you yella skunk!"

"Thanks mister, I reckon I owe you." I replied. The man nodded.

"Call me Wes," he said. Big Ben Cole eyed me angrily.

"Boy, were you serious about signing on?"

"Yes sir, I sure was!"

"Well listen to this and listen good. I put up with this little shin-dig of your'n for one reason. Seth an Ike wronged you, and if it hadn't been for that, you would have had me to deal with! Give me any trouble, and I'll call you out, and it won't be with a gun, either, get the point?" I looked at the big man.

"To tell ya the truth, I'd sooner tackle a grizzly, Boss! I said grinning. Ben nodded, feeling better at the compliment. I spoke up again,

"When I ride, I ride for the brand, Mr. Cole, and I'll remember what you said and leave you with this to chew on.

"Yeah? What's that?" Big Ben Cole grunted.

"There have been occasions when grizzlies have been whipped, Mr. Cole! Such as the time old Hugh Glass killed one with his bowie knife!"

"There is somethin' to what you say kid, but, you just remember, he had a knife! If he hadn't, he would have got killed!" Ben Cole grinned at me. I grinned right back at him. I was thinking that I was gonna like riding with Big Ben. He had sand! Pa always told me.

"Son, never ride with a man that's a coward. At the first sign of danger, he'll sell you out. If you've got to have a pard'ner, pick one with sand!"

In the days to come, I was to find that Ben Cole was a fair man. He showed no preference for any man when it come to riding drag. Drag was the dustiest and most unpleasant job of all nests to night head. The dust from the trail herd was choking, and it penetrated the kerchief over the face. It found its way into the lungs no matter how hard a man tried to keep it out and mixed with the sweat of your body and clogged the nose. This was also the most dangerous position to be riding.

You couldn't see ten foot around you for the dust, and injuns would sometimes ride up behind you and try to put an arrow in your back. You were all by yourself with the herd and everybody else ahead, kicking up dust and heaven help the man who shirked his job!

After a while, Ben put me to herding the cavvy, and taking the kinks out of the mean ones. My Pa's training me how to break horses came in mighty handy. Big Ben Cole asked no questions of his men, which was the western way and he was all western. He had a black, full mustache and a baleful of green eyes that asked a quarter of no man. Every man counted for what he was now, and you didn't pry unless you were ready to back it up with a gun.

Ben was big with shoulders like a grizzly and had a disposition to match. When he said move, most rannies moved! One or two that didn't move wasn't given a second chance!

The trail boss called them out to fight with their fists and they couldn't refuse without being branded for a coward. It was like seeing a one-legged man in a foot race. They would hit Ben square, and he'd just grunt, then they'd hit him again with more effort than before. Finally, when they'd wore themselves out, he'd let them have it. They would go flying through the air and land flat on their back, colder than a well digger's behind!

He'd throw water on them, slap em on the back, tell em that was a real good fight and that he had fun., and to let him know when they were ready for another go round. Everybody would laugh, including the man who had just got licked, for he didn't want to be called out again anytime soon. I didn't blame them much either!

Ben Cole's jaw must have been made of tempered steel. I watched him real good, and decided that if I was ever unlucky enough to get him mad, I'd work on his eyes and body. A fight between men on a trail drive was rough and tumble, with no holds barred. Anyway you could put the other man out of commission, was alright, unless you picked up a rock or something, and that would more than likely get you shot! There wasn't any point system, and no rest periods. You just fought until one man couldn't get up anymore.

But me and Ben got along just fine. He was hard but his men would go through hell or high water for him! He was a symbol of their times. He was the rocking B and Texas! The men were Texans, they were proud, Texas proud!

Along about now, my clothes were getting a little rough and ragged. My shirts had holes in the elbows, and Pa's old hat was shapeless. But I wasn't in any worse condition than most of the men. All of us were a reg-tag looking bunch. But nobody ever criticized us in any of the trail towns we passed or stopped in. Not unless they were good with a gun or their fists. Loyalty ran high on the Rocking B. If you whipped one, ya hat to lick em all! Not all at once, but one at a time. If you were a stranger, that is. If you worked for the brand, no body interfered.

It was the spring of eighteen seventy three, and the land was still fresh and new. The long grass rippled in the wind and it was good to be alive! I looked at the white clouds floating in the bluest sky I'd ever seen, and it was grand, just grand! The longhorns bawled, and sometimes buffalo would go pounding away through mud. It rained during the morning, and dew sparkled on the grass in the evening sun. I took off my slicker and stowed it behind the cantle of my saddle. The rain had washed and settled the dust. The world was clean and fresh. The way the sun was shining the raindrops wouldn't last long. I grinned and swung my quirt at the old brindle steer with the milk eye.

"Get back in there you old reprobate!" I was feeling mighty good, even if that old steer did try to turn back for home every chance he got! I watched Antelope bobbing and bounding away, flashing their white rumps. Then they'd stop and gaze back at me with their far-seeing eyes. It would soon be time to bed down the herd. It was spread out across the valley, looking like a long, snake crawling in the sun. My old spotted Nez Perce' hoss was feeling good too. He'd snort and act like he was scared every time a jack rabbit ran.

That bite on the ear did something to him. Pa said that was the way some injuns broke their horses. They'd grab an ear and bite down on it hard, every time the horse misbehaved. It must have worked pretty good because you can't ride and fight like them injuns could without having control of your horse. They could ride and fight like they were born to it, which they were, I guess, born fighting, mostly amongst themselves over horses and hunting territory. When you had an injun mad at you, he made a bad enemy, because when it came to hating, no man could compare.

5

~ ON THE TRAIL ~

I could see Red John coming across the valley from where the chuck wagon was parked under the trees. We'd finished watering the herd, and now we were bunching them for the night. I liked ol' Red John, even though he was the one who had corralled me back yonder by the creek. I was still fond of him. He was a good man, and was square as could be! He wore buckskins and a flat-brimmed hat with a feather stuck in the brim. From the markings on it, the feather was Cheyenne.

"Ok, kid, I got 'em now!" The hoarse voice of Red, rasped. "Go on in and tie on the feed bag." I looked at that old geezer kind of foolish-like.

"Are you real sure you can handle them? These critters are right out of the brush-country and dangerous. The boss might fire me if I left you all alone out here with these mean ol' longhorn cattle." Red John's mouth fell open, then it snapped shut like a steel trap.

"Huh!" he snorted with disgust.

"Easy now ol' timer," I soothed, "You're liable to bust

your belt getting' all puffed up with mad that way. I gotta take care of you and see that you don't get hurt or anything." The resulting explosion nearly spooked the Appaloosa and come mighty close to unseating me.

"Why, ya dang smart aleck, greenhorn, I been herdin' cow since ya was knee high to ah grasshopper! I don't need no wet-behind-the-ears kid, nurse maidin' me. Red John MacDonald, late of Jackson Hole, an th' black hills! Why I seen the elephant a'fore you was born, and I helped blaze th' trail yore ridin' on now! I been to rendezvous, an Coly-roddy, an'...." I grinned at him. This *'kid',* was three inches taller than Red John. I stood six feet two in my stockin' feet and weighed in at an even two hundred pounds, and there wasn't one ounce of fat on me either.

"That's just it, old timer, you've done yore work, it's time you was put out ta pasture so ya kin take it easy for the little time that ya have left!" Red John's face grew purple and puffed up like it was fit to burst.

"Why you sissifyed, upstart, of an excuse for a wrangler! Everybody knows that I ain't but forty two, an' I'm young for my age at that!" The rest of his ranting and raving went unheard as I spurred Diablo for the chuck wagon. I looked back at him as I rode, and danged if he wasn't shaking his fist at me! I grinned and waved back at him, just to make him madder. He sure was a rip-snorter and I was real fond of the old rascal and Red John liked me too, despite having such feisty outbursts of temper at my teasing.

After a big blow-in which had left most of the men broke, we headed back down the trail to Texas. Most of the men split up to go their separate ways, but we stuck with Ben, wintering in one of the Rocking B's line shacks. Our job was to help keep down the winter kill from cold and predators. The calves were brought in and nursed by a milk cow that we kept for the purpose. Most times the mother would follow us in to the line shack bawling for her calf. I was good with animals and we saved a lot of beef critters for Ben that winter.

Now it was spring, and the long trail to Abilene stretched out before us again. Most of the original crew had signed back on, too, because they liked Ben Cole. Red John liked the trail boss for the way he'd taken me under his wing. I had come from trouble, sure as you were born, but what trouble I'd never let on. Red John wasn't about to pry to find out.

"He shore is game that kid!" Red mused, and he can look lightening out of them black eyes of his when he gits mad. He had seen those kind of eyes before. It was in the winter of sixty four, and Red was flat on his back in the snow with an arrow in his shoulder.

"I looked up into that Cheyenne dog soldier's eyes and I saw death as certain as little injuns make big uns! That injun was a-straddle my chest and he screamed like a devil. He raised his war club to dash out my brains. He would have too, if ol' Chris hadn't drilled him plumb center! The big forty four caliber slug from Chris's hawkens struck the redskin in the face and blew out the back of his head. Red John had two souveniers from that day, the eagle feather in his hat and a stone arrowhead. John felt of his shoulder. He still carried the arrowhead in his flesh and it ached sometimes. When it ached, it seemed like injuns weren't very far off.

"A bad sign," Red John said to himself, "a sure sign of injun trouble." He rubbed his shoulder, there, it was paining again. He looked up at the sky. It wouldn't be long until the moon rose, then it would be almost as light as day. Red didn't like it. Maybe there were injuns about, and it was a moonlit night. Cattle got nervous during the full moon and they would stampede at the drop of a hat. He shook his head.

"Bad sign,' he said. "That foolishness about injuns not fightin' at night was hogwash. Injuns called the full moon the hunter's moon, and that takes care of that! Night was the perfect time to steal horses and count coup on a living enemy while he slept, too."

"Injun's aint fools!" John added. "Their chances were better in the dark just the same as any other man's would be. That business of being afraid of dyin' in the dark, and their spirits wanderin' forever in darkness wasn't true. Why, the Milky Way was their path to the happy huntin' ground. They called it the path of stars. They believed their spirit traveled along it, and the stars were their friends. They could talk to the stars as they walked along to meet their red brothers on the other side."

"Besides, no brave went into battle until his *'medicine'* was good, and he believed himself fully protected. The signs were what they listened to. If they were good, they went ahead with what they intended to do. But if the signs were bad, they'd quit cold. The hoot of an owl was a bad sign, a sign of death. Many an old mountain man had saved his life by imitating the hoot of an owl. Of course, it had to sound genuine, for injun ears were sharp and could tell unless it was perfect."

'Old Chris had been some proficient at hooting.' Red remembered. *'He was real good at it, too. Better'n me,'* he thought. *'John never could get the hang of it.'* He worried until he heard the noise over by the river… *'An owl, a dad-burn, wonderful, sweet ol', hooty-owl,'* Red smiled, *'No attack tonight!'* Then his shoulder pained again. *'Dang it,'* There it was again, *'Injun sign!'* He wished old Chris was here. The last

time Red saw old Chris was at a rendezvous in Jackson Hole, Wyoming. I sold all my plews and left old Chris at rendezvous, still raisin' a ruckus! Red grinned.

"That old mountain man was somethin', old Chris, dancin', an' yellin', with all them grizzly claws ah clickin' an' ah clackin'! Ol' bear claw Chris lapp!" Red John laughed. Then the owl hooted again, closer this time. Red listened. Which sign was right, or were they both right?

"Easy cows," he breathed, as he circled the herd. He could hear Harvey, one of the other punchers singing low to the cattle. *'Good,'* Red thought. *'Maybe it'll calm em down some. I hope so anyway!'* Maybe he should sing, too, then he thought better of it. With a voice like his, the cattle would spook and run out of the country. Well, he could hum, so he started in humming. The cattle stirred, and two or three got to their feet. Red John quit humming!

"Dang Cows! Didn't appreciate good humming! I never did like cow critters no how! Give me a good bite of buffer cow ever'time! It beats beef all hollow, an I know-fat cow from ol bull anytime!" Red thought of hump steak, just sizzling and dripping, roast buffalo tongue, and boudins roasting over red hot coals, with mushrooms an bone marrow. *'Nough of that,'* Red frowned, *'It's a long time till breakfast.'*

I turned Diablo over to the night wrangler and strode to the fire. A bubbling, blackened coffee pot was perched on the red hot stones circling the campfire. The coffee smelled good. I poured myself a cup of the black, scalding liquid. It was strong enough to walk by itself. After I finished the coffee, I poured myself another cup and then helped myself to the beans and sowbelly that cookie had fried up. Balancing the tin plate on my knee, I began to eat heartily. After two or three bites, I looked up to see Cookie standing there with his hands on his hips, glaring at me with his one good eye. The other eye had been gouged out in a fracas down in Amarillo. It must have been a mighty, mean man to gouge a man's eye out that way, I always thought!

"Well?' Cookie growled, "Does ever'thin suit yore lordship's fancy?"

"Uh-huh! Best grub this side o' the pecos!" I grinned at cookie and raised my tin cup in salute.

"Ahhh, go on with ya!" Cookie grumbled, but I could tell that he was pleased at the compliment. He sure liked to have his cookin' bragged on.

"I got some cobbler when ya git done stuffin yore face with them beans."

"What kind?" I asked foolishly.

"Apple cobbler, ya dumb cowpoke! Ain't no other kind! When I was cookie fer the Circle D down in the panhandle, the boys' allus' said that I was the best in the territory at makin' apple cobbler. I make it from dried apples and cinnymon, flavored with blackstrap molasses. Why, I see them boys nigh go crazy after apple cobbler. They cheat, steal or lie to get a piece of it." Cookie beamed." H'yar, have yourself a hunk of it. It's hot and ready for the eatin!"

I swallowed the last of the beans and took up the piece of cobbler. I shoved it into my mouth while it was still hot, burning my tongue but it was worth it. It was fine, mighty fine! Now that it was safe to reply I said to Cookie real pious,

"Cookie, this is mighty good pie, but I have tasted better. My gal back in the brush country makes it better. If you want her recipe, I'll be glad to give it to you!"

"Why, you smart mouthed, stuck up smart aleck, gimmie my pie back! Cookie reached to grab the pie but I retreated around the fire, keeping it between me and him.

All the while I was stuffing my mouth with that cobbler.

"I'll have you know that I cooked for the XIT, mister, and a bigger outfit, they ain't, now gimme my pie back!

"Sorry Cookie, that pie was so good, I seem to have eaten all of it. On second thought my gal never did make me any apple cobbler, but if she had it would have been wonderful. She could have sweetened it just by stikin' in her lil finger! That gal sure is pretty, but I got to give credit where credit is due, that cobbler sure is the best I have ever tasted!"

"Cookie, you're and angel God sent just to keep us pore cowpokes from starvin' to death." I hung my head real reverently. He didn't know whether to cut my throat or hug my neck. He wasn't sure, but maybe one smart-aleck kid was razzing him.

"Well," he said, puffing from running me around the fire, "If'n ya liked it that good, I forgive ya', but you had better watch it. You don't know how close ya come to havin' to fetch water and chop some wood!"

"Oh Lordy," I breathed, relieved. "Thanks ah' heap, cookie." I said, putting on my hat. Cookie turned back to the chuck wagon, rattling pots and pans, putting away mysterious looking boxes and jars.

A good Chuck wagon cook was hard to come by, and drew twice the pay that an ordinary drover received. The man who gave the cook a hard time was liable to draw his pay a mite sooner than he expected. Sometimes the cowhands worked cheaper than usual for an outfit just because they had the best cook. I scoured my plate and cup with sand. Cookie didn't look any too kindly on dirty plates and cups.

"If you eat out of it, ya wash it and keep it clean! Any man that doesn't keep his plate and cup clean will likely have to eat out of his hand, an' no eatin' out of the pot! Any ranny that eats out of the pot will draw his time, pronto!

"I fetched my saddle and bedroll, shook it out and hung it on a bush by the fire to dry a mite. Ben Cole sat on a blanket and looked at his tally sheets.

"Have a seat Rance," he murmered, still working on his figures. I squatted there beside him not saying anything because I did not want to disturb him. In a moment, he looked up.

"We lost a few head when we come through the breaks, but not anymore than I figured. The way I figure it, we're standin' good if we don't lose too many head crossing the river tomorrow. The Red's up more than usual because it's been raining in those far mountains that feed this river. She's risin' and the crest could come down stream at anytime. When that happens, it'll be two, maybe, three weeks before we can cross over. If we wait, we will loose mebbe five or six dollars a head in Abilene. The earlier we get there the better price we can get. But if we try to cross the river and the crest hits us, we'll lose all the cattle! Some of us won't make it across either!"

"I plan to put it to a vote. Whatever the men vote to do is what we'll do. The morning will be soon enough to decide. When it comes to a man's life, I think he ought to be able to make the decision himself. Nobody's ever crossed the Red River when she was in full flood before. She's high now, and if she doesn't rise too much before morning, I'll vote to cross her."

I studied the big man. He made every decision considering the welfare of his men.

'Ben that's mighty square of ya' and the men won't let you down. If we can cross it at all, we'll cross. You've always been fair, and we'll not be letting you down now."

"Rance, you're a good kid. I've never pried before as to why yor' not home with yor' folks, because it wasn't any of my business. I just want you to know that anytime you need anything just call on me." After I nodded in silent appreciation, Ben continued,

"I never told anyone my story, neither. It was too painful. But I'll tell you now, just in case I cash in my chips on this trip. I was married once to a lovely girl. We had a little boy and the world was all pink and rosey. Martha was beautiful and understanding, so she didn't give me too much trouble when I signed up with Lee to fight for the south. While I was gone to war, my home was burned to the ground, my wife and boy was killed. I never did catch up to the ones that did it. There weren't any witnesses, and nobody saw the men that did it."

"Renegades, they were, because neither army had any units in the area. Just renegades! What I'd give to lay eyes on them! I've got a sister in Missouri and if anything happens to me, I want you to tell her where I have been and what I have done. Back at the Ranch, I got some money in a sack. I want you to see that she gets it. Will you do this for me?"

I looked at Big Ben Cole. Now I knew what it was that tormented him when he couldn't sleep nights. Man is born to trouble, and it sure looked like Ben had, had more than his share. Most men would have turned bad, but Ben was still fair and square.

"Shore boss, I'll see to it for you, if it happens, but I can't think of anything around here that could ever do you in! You're just too darned big an' tough. More than likely it will be you that plants me!" Ben grinned.

"Boy, you're a good friend and I trust you and one of

these days you're gonna hit it big. Take my word for it. Now, lets git some shut-eye. In my sleep that night I dreamed of big blue eyes and lips that took my breath away.

The smell of coffee and bacon frying brought me half-awake. The snores of Red John MacDonald were what finished the job. Cookie was up mighty early this morning. I saw the big shadow of Ben Cole squatted by the fire drinking coffee from a tin cup. *'Doesn't he ever sleep?'* I asked myself.

"Mornin' Rance," Ben grunted as I helped myself to a cup of coffee. "River's still runnin' high but I think we can make the crossing. The men will be voting on it after breakfast. We'll be ready to go by daylight mebbe."

The voting went just like I figured. Every man-jack of the crew voted to make the crossing. This was a hard land but these were hard men, and they could handle what it threw at them. Hardship and trouble were their constant companions, and they knew and accepted the dangers.

"O.k. boys, take one man and herd the cavvy over first. Then we'll float the chuck wagon on over next. After that, we'll cross the herd. Move fast, the crest can't be too far upriver. From the way that water's movin', she's close.

I caught Red John's eye and we started swimming the horses across the river. The water was cold and muddy from the flooding. Some of the horses squealed in fright as we herded them over the river's edge. The ones in front were pushed into the water by the ones behind. Two or three tried to turn back, but Red swatted them with his rope.

"Git in thar, ya blamed crowbaits! I swatted a piebald in the rump with my quirt. All of them were in now, and we followed them splashing and swimming our horses across.

Red was just ahead of me, holding his rifle over his head to keep it dry. I did the same with my spencer.

"Keep them moving!" I yelled. Some of the horses were about to be carried too far down river. I watched the horses as they scrambled up the far bank. All of them made it! So much for the cavvy!

"Yaaaaahooo!" Red John whooped as his horse found bottom and scrambled through the shallows. "We made it! Hey Ben! When you get the wheels off of the chuck wagon, have Harvey and Jake tie on to both front axles and bring the ropes over to us. Then we kin haul her across easy!" Red John had his back to the brush on the far bank and he was looking across the river toward the herd. That's why he didn't see the injuns!

6

~ <u>INJUNS!</u> ~

Kiowas, they were, and they came sudden. There were three of them and they were racing each other to see who was going to be the first to take Red, John's scalp! I just up and plugged one of them and was drawing a bead on another one while the first one was still falling. I got that one too, but the one in front must have been eyeball to eyeball with Red, when he turned his head to see what I was shooting at. That brave brought his coup stick down on Red's head so hard his horse must have felt it. That Kiowa just galloped right on by as Red John flopped half in and half out of the water!

The brave jerked his pony around and came back hell for leather, meaning to ride his horse right over Red! Diablo had found footing, and he splashed up through the shallows throwing rocks and sand from his hooves. He was a big horse and his shoulder caught that injun's pony in the ribs, making the pony gave an audible heave from his lungs, throwing him sideways and over on his side, his legs and hooves flailing in the air.

That pony rolled clear over, and the brave that was riding him was just climbing to his feet when I laid him over the head with the stock of my spencer. Harvey and Jake were still swimming their horses across when I saw the other Kiowa's hooting and riding their horses down river towards us.

At the sight of me and the horses the injuns started really whooping it up and they headed straight for me and Red John! Harvey and Jake were across and were shooting as they rode up beside me. The men on the other side were shooting now, too. Most of their shots were going wild.

I saw one of the Indian emptied from his saddle by a bullet from Red's old needle gun. He was sitting there in the water and he was mad! Real mad! He threw down his sharps, and pulled his colt just as the Kiowa hit us. They rode right into us shooting and stabbing with their lances. We were outnumbered and I was emptying Indian saddles just as fast as I could shoot!

The spencers that Ben Cole insisted that we all carry made the difference. When mine was empty, I threw my colt just as a mean-eyed brave made a pass at me with his war club. Pa's old navy didn't, make much difference between a white man and a red one. It killed that Indian just the same.

Harvey was down holding his belly and a Kiowa fired right into his face. I shot the Indian in the spine, and lost my hat ducking another war club. It was fight or die, and no time for talking. I guess Pa was helping me because all the while I could hear him saying to me,

"Make it count, son, don't ever waste powder or lead." I don't know how many Indians were killed before the two or three that were left decided that they'd had enough. They turned tail and ran, shaking their fists and flapping their breech clouts at us. By us, I mean me, and Red John. Harvey was dead, and Jake was lying in the mud with a Kiowa lance sticking up out of his chest. He died that night by the fire. We all watched him while he lay there trying to smile up at us.

"I'll make it Ben," he gritted. "I'll be back earnin' my pay before you know it! I just need to rest a while. Somebody gimme some water? I'm powerful thirsty."

Cookie put a tin cup to his lips. He drank, and strangling red blood gushing from his lips, he cried out,

"Ma? … Ma, where's Pa? Where's he gone? He's gotta come back, he can't die, he just can't!

Jake was nineteen years old and he was a man. We buried him there beside the river where the wind whispered through the cottonwoods. Jake loved trees. He was from the Tennessee hills, where there are lots of trees and mountains to roam. It was feuding country and the men that came from there had sand!

Cookie burned Jakes name into a rough board and placed it at the head of the boy's grave. It said,

'Jake Hatcher'
'A Man!'

We laid Harvey right beside him. Harvey Logan was a man, too! It was kind of like Pa would say,

"Some men think that they're going to live forever, but everyone dies. It's better to do it honorably than to die miserably, and a coward!"

It was quiet that night around the fire. Two of our men were dead, and we'd lost a few of the cattle. It was bad bout Harvey and Jake but we had been lucky as far as the cattle. We had stood to lose more, lots more. Red John had a lump the size of a hen's egg on his head. Rubbing it and glaring at me,

"Why'd the dang redskin have to hit so hard?" Everybody laughed. Things were seemingly back to normal. I drank my coffee and stared into the darkness, listening to the coyotes. The Kiowa had come swiftly, trying for coup and scalps. They got no scalps and they got no horses, yet they left many of their braves in the tall grass. Squaws keened and moaned in the valleys and the camp dogs howled at old man death's ghostly visage.

Medicine was bad an owl hooted from the spirit world. A bad omen, an omen of death! It was a good time to stay in the teepee, and make supplication to the spirits. The man called Wes squatted beside me.

"Been meanin' to have a palaver with you Rainey, soon's we could be alone." I was surprised. Wes was a man who kept to himself. He had no close friends that I could think of, and I noticed that Ben Cole paid him the compliment of asking for his advice now and then. Wes wasn't a joking man, or one who stood for foolishness. Some of the men were plainly afraid of him.

He wore two guns, ivory handled and tied low, so that his hands brushed the grips as he walked. He was the man who'd known Pa Rainey, and well enough to hold my respect. Old Bill took few men into his confidence, and this man had known Pa's guns and his stallion on sight. He further surprised me when he asked,

"How did he go, son?"

"Bronc!" I answered and after a while he replied,

"I knew it had to have been somethin' like that! He spat, and then got out the makin's.

"Smoke?" He offered.

"Don't smoke," I said. "Thanks anyway.

"Neither did your Pa." He didn't smoke, nor drink, either. He was a good man with a gun, though. We rode together, and he was fast, real fast. He saved my life, once. At a lil necktie party held in my honor." He chuckled in his throat. The man appeared to be taking me into his confidence, and again I was surprised.I held my silence, waiting. After a while, he looked at me and said,

"Boy, word is you've killed men, but we both know some men need killin,' any man that abuses women folk deserves to die!" This man called Wes seemed to know everything about me! *Who was he and how did he know?*'

"Mister, if you know that much about me, maybe you know about my Ma and Jori Lee? Are they alright? I gotta' know how they are. Can you tell me?" I looked at him, waiting. His eyes burned like wolve's eyes and he ground out the stub of his cigarette.

"Your, folks are alright, take my word for it. I promise you that! They're being looked after. Bill Rainey helped a lot of folks and there's some would take it mighty bad if anything happened to his kinfolk. I guess we're both ridin' the high lonesome, you might say."

"Well, I'm beholdin' to you, Wes, if that's your handle. You've helped to ease my mind. I thank you for that and consider it a favor. Thanks a lot!"

"I owed it to your Pa, boy," he drawled, and he studied the ground a while before saying, "Wes is just part of my name. The rest of it doesn't matter. "But a man ought'a know who his friends are." He looked up at me and his eyes seemed to burn through me. "My name's, John Wesley Hardin, but just call me Wes."

There it was. This man was one of the most dangerous men that ever lived! He knew Pa, and Libby, and had declared himself an ally. He was now my friend in a land that didn't take the word lightly. I watched him as he faded away into the darkness, and my respect for my Pa grew a lot bigger.

It rained for the next three days and it seemed like the whole world was drowning. Everybody was wet and miserable. Tempers flaired, there had been a couple of fist fights but they were broken up by Ben. Cookie was a wonder, though. Somehow, he always found dry tinder for a fire. He stretched a tarp from the side of the chuck wagon and we hung our wet clothes from a line between the poles. The fire dried us and our clothes while we ate in shifts. It was a sight to see. Some of the men stood in their long johns before the fire, toasting their backsides.

The flour was moldy and hard but cookie gained our respect for his grub. Somehow it always tasted good. Me and Red kept the outfit in fresh meat. I thought Pa had taught me a lot but old Red John had been a mountain man. He rode the river with the best of them and he was still alive with a full head of hair.

"I knowed ol Liver-eatin' Johnson, Kit Carson, an' Jim Bridger! I trapped with some of em' and met the rest at rendezvous. Liver-eatin' was the only man to win a war single handed against a whole injun nation. The crows murdered his wife when she was with child so Johnson declared war on em'. He got his name from eatin' the livers of his enemies, the Crows."

"Those Crows picked two hundred of their best an fiercest warriors to kill him but he got em all, one at a time. Until they got smart and started to gang up on him. They captured him once, but he escaped. John Johnson was his real name. He killed so many of the Crows that they decided to smoke the peace pipe with him."

"Why'd he eat their livers, Red? Seems to me, he must have been a bit crazy, to do a thing like that."

"Back in them days, times was mighty rough, kid. A man had to be tougher and meaner than his enemies to survive. He had to eat things and do things that would turn a civilized man's stummick! I kinda figure Johnson did what he had to, to make the injuns afraid of him. It threw their thinkin' off and caused em to make mistakes. Boogered em' ya might say. He wanted them to know who had done the killin' I guess the liver business was his sign."

"The Sepulveda brothers, Bear Claw Chris Lapp, Hugh Glass, Del Gue, they was men, boy, real men. They found the passes, blazed the trails and walked where no white man ever walked before. They didn't have none of these fancy repeatin' rifles, neither! It was just powder and lead, and then cold steel! Many a man went under in them days, 'cause he couldn't reload fast enough. Ol' Betsy here, she's counted coup plenty a'gin red skins. Finest rifle in th' west, kid."

I didn't mind Red John's braggin' too much, I guess he had a right to brag. He'd known the great ones, the trailblazers. When I got to thinkin' about it, it hadn't been all that long since then, maybe ten years or so. Things were going slow now that we had crossed the red. Ben Cole was as tickled as could be with his tally. A lot of the cows had dropped calves. More than enough to make up for any losses we had endured.

"Pssst, Kid!" Red John's warning sounded loud to my ears. "Thar they be, down in th' holler there." I eased forward to peer over the rocks. At first I couldn't see them but then I could see the hump-backed shapes of the buffalo.

"Now we'll jest take it easy, kid, an' pick us out two of

them young, fat cows. They make a lot better eatin', than them ol' tough bulls. Thar! See her, by thet big clump o'bushes. Next to that ol' lightnin' struck pine. Keep yore eyes on her whilst I pick me out one. Wagh! I got 'er now, kid! Ready? One, two, three, fire!" Black smoke belched from Pa's old sharps at the same time as old Betsy spoke. Both cows dropped in their tracks.

"Wagh," John grunted, pleased. "They'll be plenty of fat cow hump an' buffler steaks tonight. Cookie will be some pleased, now won't he, kid?"

"He sure will, Red," I answered. I had already reloaded my rifle, Pa taught me that.

"Always keep your gun ready, boy, empty guns don't kill any snakes, an' you never know when a snake might be around."

"C'mon boy, lets take a look at them cows!" Red John stood up and was halfway down the hill before I broke cover. For a mountain man, John was a little sudden. I guess he was getting a little careless since his trapping days. I hadn't seen him reload his gun, either

I moved slow and careful. We were a good ways ahead of the outfit and two men could be real easy pickin's for anybody with the wrong intentions. I kept mostly in the rocks as I moved down slope.

"Hey, kid, where are ya?" John called out when he reached the buffalo. "They be fine, fat cows, Kid?"

"Here, ol' timer!" I stepped out from the shadow of a big boulder.

"What ye slippin' around fer?" John's brow furrowed as he looked around. "You feelin' spooked, maybe?"

"Easy ol' timer, I was just being careful."

"Dad burn it!" John spat on the ground. He was mighty disgusted with himself. "After all I done tol' ya' about pertectin' yer hair! I guess I'm gittin' careless in my old age, sorry, kid!"

"Don't matter none, I guess I wasn't careful enough, look there!" I pointed up the hill.

"Great jumpin' Jehosophat, kid, we're done for! That's Kiowa, shore as you're born naked! He cocked his rifle.

"No use," I whispered, "you forgot to reload!"

"Dad Burn it, again!" Red John really wasn't pleased with himself at the moment. "What'll we do kid?"

"Bluff it? They don't know whether your gun is loaded or not. "At least, I hope they don't." I squinted up at the Indians. They had come in with the late evening sun at their backs.

'No fools live long in this world,' Pa always said, and those Kiowa were not fools! I watched them as they walked their horses down the hill. The leader was short, with queer looking drooping mustaches which gave his face a kind of oriental look, like a China man. I decided that I definitely did not like the man.

"Oh Lordy," John was fidgeting like a six year old in church. "Kid, that'd be ol' Santantie himself!"

"Santana!" I had certainly heard that name before. Pa and Ma had told tales about this very Indian around the fire at home. I particularly remembered the one about the little girl. Santana had tried to sell a little white girl to the soldiers at one of the forts here about. I forget which fort it was, but the soldiers hadn't had enough guns and powder to buy the little girl. Santana held her up and disemboweled her before the soldier's eyes. A few of the soldiers had fired at the chief, but the distance was too great. Santana was out of range and he knew it. The commandant of the fort didn't dare attack, either. He was far too outnumbered. All he could do was sit and watch helplessly while Santana murdered the little girl. Some of the soldiers cried openly while they cursed the old chief. Many had been the vows of vengeance but here was the chief before me now, safe and healthy and still as dangerous as a wounded bear.

I held Pa's old needle gun casually, but its muzzle was dead on the Indians brisket when he reined in his pony. My left hand was full of colt navy forty four. A couple of braves edged around, trying to get behind us. There were four of them, all told.

"No!" John spat tobacco juice at their ponies' feet. He cocked ol' Betsy again, threateningly.

"White men kill injun's buffalo!" The chief's voice was coarse and guttural. "Spoil injuns hunt. We take!" Santana's eyes were veiled behind heavy lids.

"No!" I said to him. "We will share our kill with the red man, but we will not give up both of our animals."

"Injun mebbe kill white man," the chief hissed threateningly. "We take!"

"Then we will all die!" I looked at Santana squarely. Then I cocked Pa's sharps. Santana straightened up in the saddle. He was a dead man if any one of them opened the ball and he knew it.

"You afraid! You no give injun buffalo if you not afraid!" He grinned like a demon straight out of hell. I stepped closer, so close that I couldn't miss even if I tried. I was getting ready to lose my temper. I had to settle this one way or the other.

"I am not afraid, red man." I bared my teeth in a cold smile. "I will not be the first to die!" That was it! I'd called his hand and the next play hinged on him. He stared me in the face and scowled. Then he said something surprising.

"You injun," he asked?

"Maybe" I said, though I didn't think so. I didn't know

what bloodlines I had. My real folks could have had a little Cherokee in them, maybe. I certainly did have the looks for it.

"We no fight!" Santana motioned to his braves. They edged toward the buffalo. "We take biggest buffalo." He said shortly. I said nothing. I let him have his way as long as it would get rid of the old buzzard! The Kiowa galloped away with the prize.

"Whew!" Red John breathed. "I felt the roots of my hair pullin out the whole time! This child ain't forgettin' to reload, never agin,' kid!"

"Let's ride," I said shortly, "They might come back!" we took off for the herd and Ben Cole's boys.

7

~ <u>STAMPEDE!</u> ~

*L*ater Ben listened carefully to what I had to say about the Indians. I left out the part where John forgot to reload, as it didn't matter now. I could see him looking at me gratefully.

"It must have been old Kicking Bear's Kiowa that hit us at the Red." Ben said grimly. "If it had been Santana's braves we killed, he never would have let you boy's go like that!"   "He didn't have no choice!" Red John Broke in. "The kid here had him dead to rights. Santana ain't no fool! He didn't have no more choice o' livin' than a one-legged man in a rear kickin' contest! Just one wrong move an' he would have had sharp's lead fer breakfast!"

"Good thing!" Ben Cole had a worried look around, "C'mon and eat. I'm posting double guards tonight. So get ready quick, on the double!"

The way the boys were eating, I kind of regretted giving Santana that buffalo. Me and John were last in line, and the steak was disappearing fast. Finally, we got our share, and sat down by the lee side of the chuck wagon.

The wind was blowing, and the air was cool. The fire

flickered and danced. The smoke shifted this way and that causing some of the men to cough, and to rub their eyes.

"Shell weather before mornin'," John's beard was greasy. "We gotta watch them cattle real close. Thunder an' lightnin' will send the critters runnin' e'ver time!"

The breeze freshened out of the east, and the first drops of rain pattered around the chuckwagon's canvas.

"Git the slickers," John grumbled, "It's gonna be a wet, dark night.

"Let's go." Ben Cole said shortly. He ground out a cigarette with his heel, and then strode for his horse.

"Come on, ol' timer, we got work to do." I hid the grin on my face when John glared and set his teeth. He sure was touchy about his age.

"Boy, you call me old timer once more and I'll paddle yore backsides." I noticed the way he threw his leg over the saddle, trying to show what good shape he was in. I mounted up. Thunder rumbled in the distance.

"Coming," I mumbled. John looked pleased. "The storm I mean." I pointed towards the flashes of light in the distance.

"Oh!" John grunted. "I thought ya was talkin' bout catchin' up, slow as you was gettin' started!"

The cattle were up and standing with their backs to the wind. They were nervous, tossing their heads and lowing with apprehension.

"Bad sign," John said in my ear. The wind was getting worse every minute. "They'll run shore, if that lightenin' gits' any closer." The air was charged with electricity. Strangely enough, there wasn't much rain, just this queer, crackling feel to the air and a smell of brimstone. A glowing luminous half light gave the surrounding landscape a strange, doomsday look. I used to listen to Pa read the

Bible and everytime he got to the part about the end of time and doomsday, I'd turn my head and grit my teeth and try not to listen.

"Skerry!" John yelled at me and I nodded vigorously. Then there was a crack of lightening that sounded like ten cannons going all at once. I saw the cattle standing poised, like they were listening to something far off, then as the brightness of the flash died, the air crackled and a green fire sparkled and jumped from the cattle's horns, outlining their bodies in the darkness. The green fire arched and crackled between the wide-spread horns of a big mossy back steer.

I had seen some bad storms before, but I had never seen anything like this. Red John and his mount were covered with the fiery glow. Then a ball of lightning rolled across the ground, followed by a clap of thunder that was both ear splitting and deafening. The ball bounced and jumped rolling straight for the cattle!

"Look out, Kid!" John's shout was drowned out as the ball exploded among the longhorns. Bawls of pain and fright gave way to the rolling thunder of cattle running.

"Turn em! Quick!" I heard the deep voice of Ben's echo over the noise of the cattle. There was a flash of guns as the drovers fired right into the face of the leaders, then pitch blackness blotted out the cattle, Red John and everything!

Diablo was running hard for the front. I could feel the pounding of his hooves under me. What if he stepped into a hole in the blackness, or we come to an arroyo? The hairs on the back of my neck prickled at the thought. I could hear Red John's pinto galloping close behind me. I was listening to every sound, jumping as a long-tailed tom cat in a roomful of rocking chairs. There was another white flash, and in the light of it I could see the herd. It was turning! I

could see the leader's head bobbing and the clack of ivory
as their horns collided. Ben and the rest of the drovers had
turned the herd, but it was turning straight back to the left,
right for me and Red John! The appaloosa saw them too,
and he put on the breaks, sliding back on his haunches,
even before I could haul back on the reins. I heard the
curse of Red John, then I felt Pa's stallion go down before
the impact of the Pinto.

I rolled, trying to remember everything Pa had told me
about how to fall when a horse threw you. The horses were
all tangled up and the pinto squealed with pain as the
stallion bit him. Diablo didn't like being run down in the
dark. Red leaped up and grabbed for the horse's reins as
they came struggling to their feet.

"Whoah thar, ya spotted devil!" he shouted, trying to
pull the pinto out of reach of the stallion's hooves. Diablo
screamed with rage, reaching out with yellow teeth for Red
John. I grabbed his bridle with muddy hands, hauling back
on the horse's head and pulling it around. Even so, the
heels of the stallion drummed on the pinto's ribs before I
was up and mounted. I jerked the stallion's head back and
layed on my spurs. Red's pinto leaped forward gamely and
Red made a running mount to his horse's back.

Death thundered close behind us, as I could see the
rolling, whitened eyes of the herd's leaders. They were
within touching distance before our horses reached their
stride. One of two made it between me and Red. I felt a
blow on my leg from one of the steer's horns. If it hurt, I
didn't feel it. I was scared! Almighty scared and I wouldn't
have wanted Pa to know what I was thinking about then.

"Run you devil!" I screamed at the stallion, and I hung
on like a catamount. Every jump or so, I sank in the spurs
and yelled. Diablo laid his ears back and rolled his mean

eyes back at me. I knew what he was thinking. *Just you wait till we get out of this mister! I'm gonna take a hunk out of your hide big enough to patch a saddle blanket!'*

Most folks that have seen their old milk cows run think that cattle are slow, but they haven't seen a lean longhorn toughed by shifting for himself run. These cattle were scared crazy. Pa's stallion was holding his own, but Joh's horse was having trouble. He was losing ground. I could see him spurring and laying on the leather with his rein ends. He'd take a look back at the bobbing backs of the cattle, then he'd hit the pinto with the reins. I could see the whitness of his face by the glare of the lightening. I saw something else, too. We were coming up on a creek bed fringed with cottonwoods.

It got dark again and I got as close to Diablo's hide as possible before we hit the wash. I felt him stumble, and then we were across and over a low bank on the other side. I couldn't see it but I felt it. The cattle couldn't run forever, but it sure seemed like it with them breathing down my neck like this. The night lit up again and I saw Ben Cole cutting across in front of the cattle. Bud sawyer was right behind him ridding hard. I could see someone else behind him but I didn't recognize who it was, Wes maybe? Then I saw that Red John's pinto was running neck and neck with a longhorn, but John wasn't on him! He was back there under the pounding hooves of the cattle!

"John! Red John!" I yelled, knowing that I wouldn't get an answer. I taken out my gun and I shot down the leader of the herd as he ran. I felt the hot sting of tears as I thumbed the hammer. Another steer fell. I heard the guns of Ben Cole and Bud Sawyer. Steers fell and the cattle swung left.

"Turn em, make em mill!" Ben Cole shouted. I fired that

last shot in the navy and saw a steer stumble and fall. The cattle were circling, running around and around, bumping into each other, slowing down. The stampede was dying out. I stopped Diablo and stared back into the darkness.

"John! RED JOHN!" I shouted.

"Easy son." Ben murmered as he took Pa's colt from my hand and placed it into my holster.

"But he don't answer," I whirled on him wildly. "Red John don't answer!"

"I know, son." Ben said quietly, placing his hand on my shoulder. "I know."

It was coming into daylight by the time the cattle were bedded and me and Wes taken out to look for Red John's body. I knew that no man could survive on foot before a stampede like the one we had just experienced. Wes rode silently, not saying anything. I had shed tears before the men and I felt ashamed. Everybody seemed to find something that took their attention, like the ground or the clouds in the sky. Nobody said anything. I guess one look at my face was enough to convince them that I wasn't feeling too kindly toward the world.

Ben didn't say anything when I said that I was going looking for Red John. He just nodded and said,

"Go with him, Wes." I saw the look that passed between them. It said, *'Look out for the kid.'* The ground was trampled into a muddy mass of tracks and debris. We came to several calves and crippled animals. These we put out of their misery, but there was no sign of Red. I dreaded what we might find, but I had to look. Here the stampede had split to go around a large rock or tree, and here the pounding, pushing bodies had flattened the brush.

Just off to the side was a prairie dog town. The little animals whistled at us as we passed, then darted into their tunnels. If only the stampede had just gone a little more to the left.

I had my mouth set in a hard, straight line as we came up to the streambed where I had last seen Red John McDonald. That old man had been my best friend, and a man should look after his friends, Pa always said. I'd left the stallion with the cavvy and was riding, a buckskin mare that Ben let me use as one of my riding string. She wasn't as big as Diablo, but the mare was a fine saddle horse with dark stockings, dapples and had a clay coloring. She was half quarter horse and half Morgan, a typical, steady, stock horse.

I walked her to the wash and stopped. She snorted and laid back her ears. The buckskin smelled blood! I took my spencer and left her ground hitched. Wes was right on my heels as I slid down in to the wash with my heels digging in.

"Well, h'its about time, some of you, dad burn tender feet was showin' up!" Red John stood spread-legged over a beef carcass, a dripping cut of meat in his hand. He pointed at the steer with his blade and sunlight glinted from the green river knife that he always carried. It was one of John's most prized possessions. "I was gettin' hungry a waitin' fer ya!" I grinned at the old cuss.

"Appears to me like a real sure as shootin' mountain man shouldn't be fallin' off his horse and getting lost all the time! Everybody knows that a mountain man doesn't have to eat but once a week or so! Ain't that right, Wes?"

"Well, Rainey," Wes winked at me, "if I ever meet up with one of 'em, I'll ask him. I don't know too much about mountain men, just that all of 'em are ugly, mean and contrary as a sore-tailed tomcat! They eat their meat raw, too, I hear tell!" I heard the whistling intake of breath as Red John's boiler busted and blew sky high.

"Why, you dad-blasted pair of grinnin' jackalopes, if it had been one of you, greenhorns, on that fool turtle of a horse last night, you'd probably have stuck with it, and got killed for your foolishness. Me, I got off that slow plug of a cowpony the first chance I got. I grabbed hold of that there cottonwood limb over there before I was killed!" He pointed at a low limb that branched off of a giant cottonwood growing on the opposite bank. The trail of the stampede passed directly under it. *Lucky!* I thought to myself, '*mighty lucky!*'

"That sure is a tall tale that you're telling there, Red, I don't know as a man your age could catch hold of a limb like that one at a gallop. What do you think, Wes?"

"Odds are a'gin' it," Wes stated soberly. "He probably just fell off because he couldn't ride he was so scared. He deserted his hoss leavin' it to the mercy of them longhorn critters!"

"Huh!" That dang crow bait of a pinto give out on me. If I hadn't run into that limb, I'd be food fer tha buzzards and ants. This child ain't herdin' no more cattle after this trip, I'm tellin' ya, not never, no more!" Now I'm gonna eat my breakfast, and I ain't gonna eat it raw either!

Me and Wes agreed with John about that little matter of breakfast, seeing as how we hadn't eaten since yesterday. We built a small fire, ate two steaks a piece, and then we went hunting Ben's cattle. After rounding up as many as we could find, we started to the outfit. We held the cattle where they were for two days, gathering in the strays lost in the stampede. Cookie jerked the beef from the ones that we had to kill.

"We'll leave for Abilene in the morning, so get em bunched up and ready." Ben was irritable. The stampede had cost him cattle, and cattle were money in Abilene.

"Take it easy boss, we're still ahead of the game. We're the first herd on the trail this spring, and those cattle buyers are gonna be climbing all over each other to buy your beef. "Why you're gonna be a rich man!" I grinned at the way Ben brighted up at Cookies words.

"Shore," he said, "Your right, Cookie. Let's get them moving at first light. We can't wait any longer. Some of those other outfits might catch up and get all the money." I helped myself to a cup of coffee, watching the poker game that some of the boys were playing. There was a little money in the pockets of the drovers, so the pots were skimpy. But the men played as if it was a matter of life or death.

A saddle blanket was spread on the ground. The smell of wood smoke and sage stung their nostrils and the senses. The sky was high and blue with a few white clouds just drifting along.

"Its days like this that makes a man glad to be alive, aint it, kid? I was a man that loved nature. I liked the free, wild country where the beaver splash, the trees grow tall and green. Where the smell of pine and the clear crisp bite of mountain air makes you glad to be alive." Red John sighed wistfully. "Kid, ya oughta smoke a pipe, settle your nerves and helps ya to appreciate life."

"Maybe, when I get old and senile, I'll sit around smoking one of those things, think about old times and how to stretch the truth a lil. Pa would say that when a man was lyin', that he was 'stretchin' his blanket'! I guess your blanket tore in two a long time ago, Red!" I grinned at him. He sputtered, getting red in the face. He jerked the pipe out of his mouth and glared at me.

"Don't do that!" I said.

"Huh?" Red John was puzzled. He didn't know what

was going on.

"Put that pipe back in your mouth and smoke it some more, quick!" I waved my hand at the pipe.

"Why? " John was suspicious.

"You're getting all worked up. Smoke that thang some more so it'll settle your nerves!"

"I know'd it," John flailed his arms at me. "Ya danged, twisted, grinnin', varmint, put em up, I'm agonna show ya how to talk to your elders, put em up!" I couldn't put em up as I was too weak from laughing at John's beard. When he got mad, it always bobbed up and down, looking like a running buffalo.

I ran around to where the poker game was going on to keep from being punched in the kisser.

"Want in kid?" Bud Sawyer asked me, smiling like a snake charming a bird.

"I got nothing to bet," I hedged, spreading my hands. "What about that spotted horse of your'n?" Bud smirked. "I'd like to fork that mean actin' hunk of horseflesh, sho' em' who's boss!" He grinned a smirking grin, looking to see if the other drovers were hearing him. Bud had a smart mouth. I didn't like him and he knew it.

"If ya ever want to fork that particular horse, and show him who's boss, I guess you'll have to fork me first, and show me who's boss!" I looked at him steadily, the dislike showing in my eyes.

"Why, you!" Bud started to his feet, laying down his cards.

"Forget it." Wes put a hand on Bud's arm. "This is a big pot here, Sawyer, and if you got as good a hand as you say, you don't want to miss it."

"Well, ok." Bud picked up his hand. I'll catch ya, later, Sonny." He said, with emphasis on the 'Sonny'.

"Maybe," I drawled, leaning against the wheel of the chuck wagon. Harry Longstreet was playing his guitar, and I listened, enjoying the soft gentle Spanish tune he was playing. His Spanish music always stirred my blood. Red came to stand beside me, still smoking his pipe.

"Kinda makes you think of red skirts and black eyed senoritas, don't it?"

"I ain't ever been to Mexico." I answered. To tell the truth, I was thinking of blue eyes and smooth black hair. I loved that girl, Jori Lee, terrible bad.

"John, if you're ever down in Texas, look up my folks. There's only my Ma and Jori Lee down there and I worry some about how they are makin' out."

"Why ain't you there, instead of here?" John asked. I looked at him and I knew that I had to tell him. I'd carried it too long, and I was busting to get it off my chest.

"C'mon over here where we're out of earshot,." I led the way over to a place in the shadows. It would be getting dark soon.

"Now what's on your mind, Kid?" John drawled.

"John, I reckon you're my best friend, even though I tease ya at times, just to see ya get mad. But I'd stand for you against trouble anytime, you hear?"

"Heck, I know that, kid!" John put his hand on my shoulder. I told him the whole story.

"That's why I can't go home just now, Red. As soon as I can, tho, I'm going back, but if you're ever in that country, look after Ma and Jori Lee, will ya?"

"Shore, son," John promised, "I think maybe I'll be moving down that way after we git these critters to Abilene. I'll check on your folks and look after 'em till ya get back home."

"Thanks John. I'd do the same for you, I reckon ya

know that.

"Shore, Kid. I know that, besides, I owe it to ya; you saved my life back there on the red. I a'llus pay my debts, and keep my word. Long's I'm alive, that is."

8

~ <u>CARDS AND GUNS</u> ~

"*D*ang it!" Bud Sawyer's voice was loud and rang with irritation, "lost again!" He rose, stomped off to the water barrel, dipping himself a drink, and then stomped back to the game, his spurs jingling the whole trip. "Luck's bad, but mebbe' she'll change." He grumbled, glaring at the other players.

"Por nada, compadres," the strangely soft voice of Manuel Dacordova purred with pleasure. "Eeet ees only that theee luck, she ees ah lady, and Manuel, he ees one ver' fine ladies man, si?" He laughed softly. Bud Sawyer glared at the Mexican.

"Deal the cards, and quit braggin'!" He spat on the ground sarcastically. The greasy cards fell from the Mexican's brown fingers expertly. Spangles and conchoes adorned his breeches, and a pair of silver Chihuahua spurs jingled as he threw them in the pot. Manuel was winning, and the drovers were of a mind to quit the game. But those silver spurs were coveted by all the drovers, so they stayed, matching the bets of Manuel. He knew that where the clink of gold failed to tempt them, the spurs would succeed. They were worth far more than the whole pot, but Manuel was a skilled poker player. According to Red, who recognized the Mexican, Manuel had been a dealer in one of the saloons in Texas.

"He doesn't know me, but I know him. He's a card shark an' a quick man with a gun. He killed two fellers down in Tascosa. The sheriff horned in and got hisself a grave in boothill for his trouble. Whoever plays cards with him is just askin' fer trouble."

I covertly studied the Mexican. A sombrero dangled from a braded strap around his neck. Tauseled black hair framed a face both young, and wild. His black eyes glittered above white teeth flashing as he raked in the last and largest pot of the game.

"Ah! Senores, Manuel, he ween agin!" The musical sound of his laughter was drowned out by the outraged roar of Bud Sawyer.

"That does it," Bud furiously burst out. "There ain't nobody that could win that many hands in a row and play it straight! Manuel, you crooked greased snake, fill your hand!" Cards and money fell to the ground unheeded as the men leaped up, swiftly backing away to leave the two men crouching and ready to draw their guns upon each other.

"Now, hold it right there!" Big Ben Cole roared. In his hand, his judge colt was cocked and ready for business. "I told you waddies that you could play as long as you played peaceful, but now I'm regretting it. No more poker until we get to Abilene! Now get on out and relieve Harry, Manuel and you, Sawyer, hit the sack because I'm putting you on the night shift!"

Muttered complaints from the men went unheeded as Ben glared, hovering over the two men. Manuel considered the trail boss, wondering if he could beat him even with a gun in his hand. He changed his mind, though, when he saw me loosen the thong over the hammer of Pa's colt. Red John had his sharps in the crook of his arm, the sound of it cocking was clear. Wes lit a cigarette, blew out the match, dropping it in the dust, his palm dropped over the ivory butt of his right, six gun.

"Ben's right, Manuel, settle it later, someplace, Abilene, maybe." He smiled at the Mexican. Manuel was not a fool. Ben Cole had many friends, and Wes was one of them. There was also, me and Red, Cookie, and just about the whole outfit loved Ben, except for Sawyer. He was only stuck on himself. A man could get shot to dull rags real easy if he moved too sudden. Manuel nodded to Wes, turned to stare at Sawyer, then he smiled, flashing his white teeth again.

'Thees greased snake, he weel see you een Abilene, Senor, yes?" Bud stood with spread legs, his thumbs hooked in his gunbelt.

"Shore, greaser, I'll see ya thar!" he laughed harshly. Blonde and ruddy, Bud was a typical cowhand. His face was flushed with anger and his blue eyes were shadowed by a flattened, bent crowned Stetson. He wore cowhide chaps and scuffed boots with a hole in the soles. A yellow bandana was knotted around his neck, and the plaid shirt he wore was jagged at the elboes.

Bud rode for thirty a month, but despite his temper and his conceited ways, he rode for the brand and he was proud, Texas proud.

"You waitin' for something Sonny?," Big Ben quirried. He moved forward a step or two. Sawyer grinned pleased with himself.

"Sho, boss, I'm goin, I'm goin!" he spread his hands placatingly, and then walked off whistling, *'Oh Suzannah.'* He thought that he had shown himself a big man before the drovers, but no man who's good with a gun is gonna hook his thumbs in his gun belt unless he figures the other guy is almighty slow! The way I saw it, Bud Sawyer had been about to die. He'd bitten off more than he could chew unless I missed my guess. That Manuel had all the earmarks of a sidewinder and then some, no doubt about it.

I spread my bedroll next to Ben Cole's blankets. I had stood my turn at drag with the rest of the men and soon Ben had put me to breakin' in some of the wilder stock in the cavvy. He raised my pay to forty a month because of the extra work breaking the horses. Ben had never questioned me about my past and I didn't volunteer anything. So far, I hadn't seen any wanted circulars with my name on them. But any day now, it could happen, maybe in Abilene. It probably wouldn't mean much, though.

Abilene was a wild town. A week or maybe two, and we'd be there. I'd know then if I could go home or have to ride the owl hoot trail for the rest of my life. I missed ma and my girl, Jory Lee. I studied the stars, wondering if maybe Jori was looking at them at the same time, wondering where I was and what had happened to me. *'Maybe she ain't, though. Maybe she's met some other handsome fellah and gone and got married.'* I thought to myself. "She'd be most eighteen now. Girls fell in love a lot at that age an' usually had found 'em a husband"

"Huh?" Ben mumbled in his sleep. 'What'd ja' say?' I must have spoken my thoughts out loud before I realized.

"Nothin', boss, go on back ta' sleep, now." I lay back, thinking about my girl. *'No, she ain't married,'* I reassured myself. "She promised, and she wouldn't lie to me, no how!' It burst out again before I thought.

"Huh? Whazzat? What's matter?" Ben Cole rolled over and looked at me.

"Oh, it's nothin', Ben. I was just talkin' in my sleep."

"Well, quit! Let me go to sleep, will ya?" he said, put out.

"I don't know how you can sleep with that going on." I chuckled. Red John snored, his breath whistled as he exhaled.

"Oh Lordy, what did I ever do to deserve this?" Ben moaned, "a kid that talks in his sleep, and a broken down old mountain man that snores like a bull buffalo. Each on either side of me! It's just too much. I can't stand it!" He turned over and after fighting his blankets, he was snoring almost as loud as Red.

Wes's bedroll was empty. He was on night herd, and I was to relieve him at midnite so I figured I had better try to get some sleep. I closed my eyes, only to waken with Wes shaking me awake, again.

"Time to play cowpuncher, Rainey," he chuckled. "Good luck," he said as I crawled out, staggering toward the fire and the ever present coffee pot. My boots were wet and clammy. The night seemed to grow darker as I rode the buckskin out toward the herd. Dawn would be long coming, and the night would be colder just before dawn.

As long as dawn was coming, it was still worth it. The sky began to grow lighter until I could see the black outline of the rolling hills. The stars were twinkling, fading out before the coming of a greater light, the sun. First the spearing shaft of reddish gold split a deep cleft, between the hills. More and more of the fiery fingers of light appeared, giving way to a red and gold disk that tumbled upon the crest of the hills. The whole of the universe seemed to burst open. The sounds of the night gave way to the sounds of the day.

The birds singing announced the morning almost like

they woke up all at once, singing feverishly. Now, I could see movement in the camp. When Red John came to relieve me, I only grunted,

"It's about time. Did you save me any breakfast, or did you eat it all?" John refused to be bothered, though.

"Well, hain't she a bee-you-tiful day, kid?" he said. Smoking his pipe, he gazed at the morning with blissful eyes. Every now and then, he'd sigh. I stared at him until I felt my stomach begin to rumble, so I headed in for the chuck wagon. The morning was chill, so I squatted up real close to the fire whilst I ate. Most of the men were finishing up their meal.

"Hurry up, now, boys. We gotta make time up the trail." Ben was everywhere at once. He bothered Cookie so much about hurrying until the old geezer put his hands on his hips and glared back at the trail boss.

"Ok, ok!" Ben backed off, grinning, "I'm gone, Cookie. Just take it easy!" he said, winking at me. Ben mounted his bay and rode out to the herd. I drank the last of my coffee, and then I cleaned up my tin plate and cup, putting them back in the chuck box. Me and the boys that had been on the last shift would have to catch what rest we could in the saddle.

I had just taken out at a fast walk toward the cavvy, when I heard the angry scream of a horse.

"Diablo!" I cursed under my breath as I hot footed it toward the sound.

"Sawyer!" I yelled with anger making my voice hoarse. I saw the bloody whelt across the face of my spotted horse and my anger blinded me. Sawyer swung the rope again as the stallion reared trying to trample his tormentor.

"Sawyer!" the sound was barely out of my throat as I lunged at the man. Sawyer whirled, and I caught the full force of his rope across my shoulder. The pain was sharp, excruciating. My weight took Sawyer off his feet. The force of my charge carried me clear over the man and I sprawled and rolled. Sawyer was up and rushing. He kicked a boot at my face. Catching his boot as he kicked, I twisted and hooked my spur behind his other leg, throwing him to the ground. I was on my feet, waiting, as he got back up.

Again, he rushed me but this time I sidestepped and caught him over the eye with a left. I smashed his nose with my right, driving him to his knees. While he ducked his head whimpering, he picked up a fist full of dirt and flung it in my eyes as he straighted up. He caught me then, with a right, while kicking for my groin. His boot crunched into the inside of my thigh as I turned to avoid the blow. He led with his right again and I grabbed the sleeve of his shirt. His fist shot past my face. I pulled, jerking him half around while punching him in the kidneys.

His face turned gray and he wretched.while I back handed him across the mouth. This smashed his lips. I slapped him with my open hand. His head rolled from side to side as I slapped him a couple more times. Swinging at me with his left, he failed to connect but resorted to digging his nails into my face, scratching at my eyes. This angered me so much that I lost control.

I chopped down across his arms, knocking his hands from my face. Jabbing him, once, twice, then felt his teeth, go as I brought a whistling right over my shoulder into his already smashed lips. I don't know how many times I hit him, but I heard the gallop of a horse, then a crushing weight bore me to the ground.

I had Sawyer's throat in my hands choking him when my own wind was cut off. Ben Cole's voice thundered in my ear.

"Let em' go, kid, let em' go. You're killing him, you fool!" Ben had his great arms around my neck and I felt myself going down, wheezing for air. Finally, the need for air overcame my anger, and I released my hold on Sawyer's throat. He was blue in the face.

"Is he dead?" Ben asked Cookie. Cookie bent to examine the man, and then he shook his head.

"No, but he shore don't like very much, boss. He ain't gonna be much good for a day or two." Cookie looked at me. "Boy, you are sure hell on wheels when you get riled. You better, watch that temper of yours, else you're gonna kill somebody someday. It might be the wrong person, too." Ben still had me by the neck.

"Ok, Rainey, what was this all about? If I turn you loose, are ya gonna be peaceful?" I couldn't answer. I didn't have enough wind.

"Turn em' loose boss," Cookie burst out, "Can't ya see he's chokin'?" Ben turned me loose and I fell to my knees. I held my hands to my throat, gasping for air.

"I reckon I seen it all, boss." Harry Longstreet said. "Sawyer here, tried to ride the kid's hoss, but the hoss wasn't havin' none of it. He knocked Bud, saddle an all plumb back in the brush. Sawyer got mad and started whipping the stallion. Rainey here, he jumped Bud for it."

"That true?" Ben quried.

"Yeah!" I croaked. "He hit my horse, the low down sorry buzzard!" I glared at Sawyer, who was beginning to show signs of life, he rolled over wheezing.

"Rainey, Ben said to me, I don't blame ya for defending your horse. But now, Sawyer can't ride. You'll have to double up to make up the difference. I don't want no more trouble do ya hear?" I just looked at him and gritted out,

"Nobody, hits my horse, Ben, nobody hits my horse!"

Suddenly, I realized I was calling Diablo my horse! I hadn't thought of him as mine before. He was always Pa's Stallion. Now he felt like mine, and nobody was gonna take him away from me, either. Maybe it was because he had been Pa's that I loved that horse so much?

"Throw Sawyer in the back of the wagon!" Ben ordered, "let's get movin' pronto!" He stalked off, still grumbling to himself. Red John was waiting for me when I rode out to the herd. He expectorated, rolled his chew around in his jaw, closed one eye and raised the other eyebrow, turned and stated to me matter of factly,

"Knowed it was comin', you an Sawyer. 'Course I didn't know you was gonna half-kill the varmint. Boys say they hain't much left of 'em. I can't say as I'm sorry, Christmas, fer the lickin' ya give him." John liked to call me Christmas Kid, because of my birthday. I didn't like it, since it reminded me of being an orphan, of being found at Christmas after my real Ma and Pa was killed, but I kept quiet about it.

If a man let these waddies know that something rankled him, they wouldn't show him any mercy. They callin' me, *'Christmas'* was enough as it was. John coughed, and then he growled a half good-naturedly,

"Ya better watch him, kid! Sawyer didn't like ya before, but now he is gonna hate ya. Keep yore eyes peeled son an' yore gun loose!"

Seven days and four hundred miles put the outfit in sight of Abilene, Kansas. It had been a long, hard trail and the men were ready to *'buck the tiger'* and *'see the elephant'*, as Red put it. It was getting on toward real darkness but we were almost there. We could see the glow of lights against the Kansas sky. There was a noise like the sound of firecrackers going off in the distance. Just one or two at first, then a lot of pop's and bangs mixed together.

"Hear that, kid? Them's gunshots! Abilene ain't changed none, by jingo, she was ah hell town when I first seen her an' she's still, rip-snortin' fer shore! Seein' the boss on his way over to us Red announced,"Here comes Ben! Git ready, Kid, This hyer town's one a body never forgets," Red John chuckled and added, "Shore! "

"Kid!" Ben stopping his horse beside mine, instructed, "Leave these critters to tha rest of these bow-legged cowpokes an' come with me. We'll ride on in and spot us an empty corral or two for the herd."

"Sure boss," I grinned at Red. "Bye Pappy, see you in Abilene." Red's mouth popped open. He glared, shaking his fist at us as we took off at a gallop and yelled,

"I take it all back, Santy Claus wouldn't bring nobody sech ah ill-mannered brat! Christmas Kid, huh!" Ben grinned over at me,

"Touchy ol' cuss, ain't he?"

"He shore is!" I returned. "I guess it's from eatin' all that raw meat that them mountain men eat."

"Yeah," Ben laughed. "That's it!"

The cattle pens were situated southeast of the town. Some had a few cattle in them, but nearly all stood empty because of the earliness of the season. We ground hitched the horses and waited for the herd to come up.

"Git in thar ya dad-burned, Texas, brush-poppers, Hyaaah!" Harry Longstreet slapped a steer across the rump with his lariat. Immediately upon closing the gates, the men charged Ben and me with a rousing rebel yell.

"Three cheers fer Ben Cole and' Texas! Yippeeee!" Ben smiled, and then he grew sober.

"Boys, you'all did me a real good job, and I'm mighty grateful. I'll sell the herd tomorrow and give you all a bonus. As for now, I'm buyin'!" Loud Cheers burst out as the men charged the nearest saloon. The batwings were nearly swingin' off their hinges.

9
~ ABILENE ~

"*S*et em up, bartender!" Ben shouted. "There are my men, and we're all from Texas!"

I bellied up to the bar with the rest of the drovers. But I felt guilty. I was half expecting Pa's voice to boom out with indignation at what I was doing, so I ignored the glass of whiskey that was placed before me. The piano was deafening and even though only a few herds had come up the trail so far, the town was crowded. One of the dance hall girls pushed in between me and Ben, giving me a great big professioned smile as she fingered the hair at nape of my neck.

"Hi, Sonny, my names Flo, what's yours, sweetie?" Not likin' her touching me, I just grunted and tried to ignore her.

"Name's Christmas, we call him the Christmas Kid! Red John snickered gleefully. He paid no mind to the fierce glare I gave him, but just kept right on, flappin' his jaw which was the old geezer's main talent. "He wasn't bornded like other folks but was brung by Santy Claus!" Flo giggled, and the other drovers snickered. There's no telling what else Red might have told her if it hadn't been

94

the little interruption that happened right about then.

Suddenly, there was gunfire out in the street! Slugs smacked the windows, breaking the back bar mirror. They buzzed around over ears like mad bees. I hit the floor hard, and I had plenty of company.

One of the men sitting at the poker tables grabbed at his chest. He reared straight up, overturning the table and its contents, falling backwards into the lap of one of the dancehall girls, who was sitting in the lap of another gent. The girl screamed shrilly and then she fainted dead away, with the dead man lying across her. The man in whose lap she'd been sitting swore, voicing the opinion's of us all.

After a few more shots the bat wings opened and several men pushed into the saloon, dragging a man's body like a sack of grain. Blood trailed the group in a wet, glistening smear.

"Set em' up, bartender, gonna celebrate, pronto!" The man speaking was big, burly, with a mustache to match his filthy beard. The bartender came up from behind the bar slowly, unsteadily. Then everybody was rising up, brushing themselves off, and looking uncomfortable to say the least.

"Well, there he lays, tha sorry lawdog. He's my first, but he won't be the last!" The bearded man boasted, giving the unlucky corpse a kick.

"Aww, ye hadn't oughta kick a dead man like that, mister, even if hc was a lawdog," complained one bystander. Dirty Beard laid him over the head with his Colt, and laughed when he went down into the sawdust. Nobody else made a move. I had a mind to take a hand, when Ben Cole and Red John casually boxed me in.

"Never mind Kid," John whispered. "T'aint yore affair." I looked at him angrily. Ben Cole shook his head.

"Red's right, happens all the time here in Abilene."

"Yeah," Red whispered in my ear. "Welcome to Abilene, Kid!" I looked at the body of the sheriff. A blind man could see that he had been shot in the back!

Abilene was a tough sort of town. It was a wide-open, roaring, hell town where a dollar could get you anything from a woman to a slit throat. The piano never ceased their tinny renditions of *'Buffalo Gal'*, *'Oh Susanna'*, and *'Sweet Betsy from Pike'*. Red-eye whiskey flowed at exorbitant prices, and the cribs below the tracks did a thriving business. Guns roared and men died. This went on for twenty four hours a day. Fortunes were won and lost at the gaming tables. Faro, Poker, Rhoulette, Blackjack, Monte, you name it, Abilene had it.

Many a Texan woke up in the alleys sick and broke, with his hard earned cash warming the pockets of some tin horn gambler or two bit dancehall gal. Those that was lucky! Those that weren't didn't wake up! The false front saloons have their legends, *'The Red Dog'* and *'The Emporium'*. Abilene was a cow town, thriving on the cattle herds that came up the trail to 'Rail City'. On the southeast side of town were the stockpens, flanking the railroad which ran east and west.

Cattle buyers dickered with the trail bosses for beef on the hoof. Beef was gold, and the town liked gold. But it didn't like Texans! The Texans were wild, young and determined to have a good time. They descended on the town like wolves, howling and shooting. Signs were riddled, and windows were smashed. "Pilgrims" danced to the tune of a colt forty-four, and sometimes toes were lost or even a leg.

Red eye whiskey dulls the shooting eye and accuracy suffers. Women and liquor, fightin' and shootin', all of this was the entertainment of the cattle drover, half-wild with loneliness and tired of enduring thirst and wilderness. The young Texans drank to the bursting and saw that the willing women, there had plenty of attention. Few were the men who could come in off the trail and endure the temptations of the town without succumbing.

Jori Lee saved me, though, I reckon. Every time I looked at one of those dance hall girls. I thought of her, and some of them even reminded me of Libby. Her blonde hair all wild and touseled, those blue eyes flashing with temper. Pa was hard put to stand his ground sometimes, I guess. It seemed like I'd never get Pa or his teachings out of my mind. I couldn't get drunk, and my love for my girl kept me straight the other way. I just kind of followed Ben and Red around, even though many of the girls tried me out. Soon they left me alone, though.

"Poor stiffs in love," I'd hear 'em say. "He's crazy if you ask me!" After a while, I rode on back to the camp and palled around awhile with Cookie. I spent the night underneath the chuck wagon thinkin' about Abilene. There wasn't a decent place there to sleep. Never sleep in a room above the bar, was advice not to be taken lightly. Drunken drover's had the habit of emptying their six guns into the ceilings, and men died in their beds from lead poisoning. The town elected lawmen only to have them shot down in the streets!

Beef and gold, the town liked both, but it didn't like Texans! Clay Allison, Bill Longly and Black Jack Ketcham were just a few of the Texas gunmen that hated lawmen and Yankees, not necessarily in that order. Spend your money and get out! This was the town council's message to the Texan's. The only trouble was getting a sheriff that could enforce these ultimatums .

On the north side of town were the respectable homes

and businesses. Handbills along the tracks declared the north side of town as off limits to the Texans. Well, it was no matter to me, I didn't intend to stick around any longer than necessary. Tomorrow I'd say goodbye to the whole she-bang, good and proper.

"Don't hang around the crowd's, Son. They draw trouble, sooner or later." I had to agree with Pa. Seems like wherever there were people, there was trouble. I liked open country, where a man could be alone.

"I'm coming, Jori, I promise… I'm coming, soon." I whispered to myself. Then I was just too used to think anymore and I let the darkness of sleep cover me.

The next morning I rode into town, planning to get a bath and a shave. I'd outfit myself with some supplies and maybe see some new country farther west. I wanted to try my luck at panning gold, too.

While looking at several spare animals with the intentions in buying a pack horse, I finally decided that I would be better off with buying one of Ben Cole's string. Ben would give me a square deal and that more than these buzzards in town would do. I'd never seen such a wild broken bunch of cow tails in my life. I would be needin' to buy some tarps and packsaddles from Ben, too.

Trying to find the trail boss wasn't going to be easy, though. The boardwalks were already packed with jostling, cursing, drunken men. First tho, I'd have that bath and shave, and then I'd find Ben.

Stepping outside the emporium, I read the various signs posted on the wall. One of them in particular took my attention. It was a wanted poster with my name on it. Luckily, there wasn't much of a description. Seems like I'd become worth five hundred dollars to some folks. I left the circular alone and looked at the rest. One yellow handbill proclaimed,

"Atten:"

"All handguns are to be checked at the Marshall's office beginning at Sundown today. It shall be unlawful to carry a firearm inside the city limits of Abilene. No Texan's allowed on the North side of town, this includes all drunks, gamblers and prostitutes!"

"Warning!" This is a city ordinance and will be strictly enforced!

Signed,

J.B. Hickock, City Marshall.

P.S. Anyone leaving town may reclaim his weapon at the Marshall's office."

"Well it seems like the town council had hired themselves a new man. *'He'd better be good,'* I thought, *'good with a gun.'* I didn't see anybody that took the handbill's seriously. One and all still wore their guns, flaunting the law. Very few men gave the new Marshall long to live.

"Shore is a shame, too, 'cause he's got such bee-you-tiful yellow hair," snickered one drunken cowhand. The new Marshall was a strange looking dandy. He wore a black frock coat with a flower and a vest. A black string tie topped the vest and a gold watch chain draped across it.

I studied the new Marshall as he stalked around town posting the handbills. His flat black Stetson topped long yellow hair that fell to his shoulders. Two pearl-handled, forty-four, Russian pistols stuck out of a red sash around his waist, and his hand tooled leather boots shone, polished to a fare-the-well. *'There's something about that man!'* I wondered as I caught a glimpse of the aquiline nose with a handlebar mustache which framed his small mouth and his

pale, blue eyes. *'That's it!'* I thought darkly. *'His eyes! Cold and pale as a fish! Unnatural! Well, no matter,'* I surmised, *'now for that bath and shave, pronto!'*
I entered the building that proclaimed the legend,

'Shave and Haircuts…. Two Bits"
"Bath….Fifty Cents"

Walking through the aisles to the back, I opened the door that said, 'Bath House'. I was greeted by the sight of Ben Cole's mustaches full of soap and naked as a newborn babe!

"Well! Shut the dad blame door, Kid! You're causin' a draft, besides, them bar gals might see, dad burn it!" I laughed at the sight of Ben and his discomfiture. After our bath, Ben put his arm around my shoulder.

"Son, Ah'm gonna give you the pack horse and that little buckskin mare that you've been admiring to boot! You're a good kid, and anytime that you need a job or a meal, well, just come on down to the Rocking B. We made real good time up the trail, and a lot of it was due to your helping extra with the horses and things. I'm obliged!"

Ben slapped me on the shoulder, almost knocking me down. "I got twenty dollars a head for the cattle and that's a right good price! That was because we got here early, ahead of the other outfits. Ah'm not forgetting the way you picked off those injuns that were making off with the remuda. If they had gotten away with those horses, we wouldn't have had any remounts. We'd have been awful late getting here and maybe we wouldn't have got here at all."

"More than likely, we would have lost the beef critters and maybe our scalps, too. So I'm throwin' in the pack saddles, along with it." The big man was in hiccups, but I knew better than to refuse his offer. He would take it as an insult and a slight.

"Thanks Ben." I murmered, "You're a good man. You've been like a father to me and I'm grateful."

"Sure, and I'm Santa Claus, too." Guffawed the big man. "You just come on back to the big Bend country with me. I'll up your pay and I'll give you a share in the profits, too, by the sam hill, I will! I need your talents breaking in some new hoss flesh for the fall drive, boy!"

"Thanks, Ben, you've been mighty good to me, but I'm hankerin' to see some new country further west." We shook hands.

"Son, take my advice and steer clear of injun territory. It's bad enough on the trail even when you've got help, but to go it alone into Sioux and Crow country is just plain crazy! All of the buffalo hunters have got those injuns as mad as hell, and most all of the tribes are on the warpath. A boy your age should oughta be shining up to some girl, and enjoying life instead of being scalped by some injun buck."

I dropped my head figuring my situation sheepishly. My face felt hot.

"I thought so!" grunted Ben. "Where's your girl, back in Texas someplace?" I nodded miserably. 'Well, that's just two things that would account for yore being here instead of there. She deserted you, or you have had trouble of some kind. Son, it isn't any of my business and I don't mean to pry. I just want you to know that you can depend on me if you ever need anything. Are you sure that you wont change your mind about that job?"

"No, Ben, I won't change my mind, but I'm beholdin' to ya. I don't have any choice but to drift." My voice was gruff. I was thinking about the wanted circular on the wall of the emporium.

"Well, take my advice and buy yourself one of those '73 Winchesters. It'll give you more firepower if you need it. C'mon now, I'll help you get your supplies and packin' done, pronto!"

I bought several boxes of forty-four ammunition and some for Pa's sharps, and one of the new seventy-three Winchester .44/40 caliber rifles, a new shirt, hat, heavy sheepskin coat, socks, and pants. While I was at it I figured I'd need a new pair of boots and traded for one of the .44 Russian pistols with black grips. The revolver was supposedly one of the most up to date, accurate weapons yet made. All in all, with my staples, it added up to a small fortune.

I barely had enough for the bill even with my savings thrown in. I pocketed the small amount of change that the clerk gave me, seventy two cents. You might say that I was broke, almost. But where I was going, your horses and your guns meant safety. They were your life and I was carrying a small arsenal; the Colt, the Russian, the Spencer fifty-six, the Winchester, and Pa's fifty caliber Sharps buffalo gun for distance. To tell the truth, I felt a little silly with all the fire power that I was carrying.

"You won't feel silly if you get in a place where you need an extra shot or two, after your first gun is empty, kid!" Ben admonished. "You take an injun charge, now, one man can't reload fast enough. He's gotta have firepower. Now, boy, here's that bonus I promised you." The first time I ever saw Big Ben smile was then.

"I can't Ben, it's too much…."

"Shut up! I've got no kin! A man needs to feel like there someone that he can give a helping hand to, once in a while. Besides, I'd like to think of you as if you were my son."

We were making the second trip outside to the pack horses when Red John came striding purposefully across the street.

"They're at it again, Boss, Manuel and Bud Sawyer, over in the Jack o' Diamonds saloon. They're gonna lock horns, pronto." Men were pouring from the saloon and lined up on the boardwalk to watch. They were followed by Bud Sawyer, red-faced and swearing. Bud stomped across the rutted street.

"Manuel, C'mon and get it, or are you yellah, too?"

The batwing doors on the saloon parted and Manuel stepped slowly out moving lazily. He stopped to light a cigar. The blue smoke billowed upward into the evening sun.

"You are eeen ah beeg hurree to diee, myeee frien'." He said, and then he moved into the center of the street, facing Sawyer who was killing drunk.

"Now you greaser, Ah'm gonna show you how we treat low down greasy snakes and tin horn gambler's down in the Big Bend!"

Manuel DeCordova faced him, smiling but the smile did not extend to his eyes. They were cold and dark, fathomless. The lazy careless face of the Mexican was deceptive.

'He's ready,' I thought. 'Loose and smooth, just like Pa said ya had to be to stop leather and live! Sawyer's gonna die.' The declaration rushed darkly down the corridor of my mind as I watched it all through narrowed eyes.

"Boss," Red John urged, anxiously, "Aint ya gonna do anythin?"

"No," Ben shook his head. "They're off my payroll, now and it's their own affair." He watched, tensely.

"Now, greaser!" Sawyer's hand grabbed, but the heavy slugs from Manuel's six guns drove him backward under the horse hitch rail. He fell heavily, the horses trampled him as they reared and stomped in fright. Manuel calmly reloaded his pistols.

"I am truly sorree, senor Ben, but Manuel takes no such words from anyee man, Si?" He smiled coldly. The tall black coated Marshall strode up. His voice was gruff and commanding.

"You're under arrest! Drop your gun belt, friend!" Manuel turned to find the Marshall confronting him. Again he flashed the cold smile.

"I think not, senor, eeet was a fair fight, an' I do not weesh to kill one so pretty, no?" The Marshall spoke with a growl.

"You are breaking the town ordinance which comes into effect as of now, seeing as it is sundown. All you men who wish to stay in Abilene will check your guns at the Marshall's office! Any man who refuses to do so will be arrested or shot, however they want it!" The blonde handlebar mustache bristled.

"No senor, I do not weesh to geeve up my guns, neither do I weesh to leave town. Manuel theenks that he weel stay, si." The Mexican pulled the butt of his fourty four. It was a bad mistake. The Marshall's arms flicked and the twin explosions of his silver guns sounded as one. Manuel's face disappeared in a spray of blood and bone! I stared, shocked at the sadness of it. The new Marshall was fast, faster than any man that I had ever seen.

"Does this man work for you?" the Marshall waved at the prostrate form of the Mexican.

"Did work for me," Ben corrected shortly. The Marshall glared.

"Then you can pay for his funeral. This town doesn't pay for any trouble maker's funeral!" Big Ben Cole stared, his jaw growing hard. Then he bristled,

"Why, you four-flushing, two bit," He started for the Marshall but I grabbed him.

"No, Ben, No! He's a killer Ben. You wouldn't stand a chance, boss!"

"I'll thrash him with my fists!" Ben roared.

"Do not bet on it, friend," said the Marshall quietly. "I do not brawl like a common ruffian, but if you wish to try, please do so," he spoke mockingly, with deadly intent. Ben finally realized what this man was paid to do by the town council, to kill Texans! The man wouldn't hesitate to shoot if Ben as much as stepped toward him. Still, Ben was half tempted to try, anyway.

"Marshall!" My voice echoed down the street as I stepped forward.

"Stay out of this, Kid!" Ben growled.

"No," I replied. "Didn't you just say that I was the same as your son? I'm making it my business! Marshall, this man is a good man and a fair man. I also know that he has no chance with you with a gun. Ben has broken no law because we're leaving town as your ordinance states, but unless you want to do as my friend Ben Cole offered, take off your guns and take him on fair and square with your fists, then you'll have to take me on too!"

'Boy, there are too many people that would very much like to see me with my guns off, as you say. No, I cannot accept your friend's offer, and my demand that the man's funeral be paid stands."

"No!" I felt my old enemy start to prickle the hair at the back of my neck. A kind of hot creeping inner heat made me answer the man shortly. "The town can take care of its own snakes!" The Marshall stared at me with his cold, blue eyes.

"I always shoot a man in the head, friend. That way when he goes down, he goes down for good!"

"Hello Bill." The voice came from our right. I turned my head slowly, keeping one eye on the Marshall. He didn't even turn his head, but just kept staring at me with those eyes of his.

"Hello, Wes." He said quietly. "Allow me to introduce my friends, Bill. This is Big Ben Cole, who's never been whipped in a fist fight and the tall one is a boy that we call, the Christmas Kid. I've seen him shoot, Bill, and I'd say that he is a shade faster than you. Of course, I could be wrong, Bill, it's been a while since I saw you last. When was it, '71?"

"Thereabouts," The Marshall grunted. "Get on with it, Wess, what are you tryin' to say?"

"Why, just that it would be foolish for you two to go at it over the Mexican's funeral. If I'm not mistaken, there's a hundred in gold in his pockets. That ought to cover the expenses, Bill. Besides, like I say, these are my friends." The Marshall didn't like it at all. Wes had him boxed, and he knew it. He gave me one more stare, and then sighed.

"Just so the bill is paid." Then he stared at me again, briefly.

"Where are you from, boy?"

"Here and there," I said.

"I got me a feelin' about you. You better do what you say and leave town, or else check in your guns. You have one hour."

"I'll be gone," I answered, not liking the way he pushed me. But there was that circular with my name on it on the wall of the Emporium, and I was leaving town anyway.

The Marshall eyed the pack horse, turned and walked away without a backwards glance.

"Thanks, Wes." Ben Cole said to the man leaning against the building.

"Welcome." Wes said around his drooping cigarette.

"See ya, Kid." He waved his hand at me as he strode off across the street. I turned to Ben.

"Boss, take my advice and hit the trail for the Big Bend! Manuel was fast, but that Marshall is lightening, and hits em' in the head, too! A man that can keep that cool and shoot that straight will sure increase boot hill's population."

"You're right!" Ben grudgingly admitted. "Besides I'd better get this gold home to some of the folks who trust me with it. The longer that I stay in this hell town, the more likely I am to be robbed or shot from the dark. Let's go!"

We mounted up and rode up the street with me leading the pack horse. Seeing the Marshall walk into a saloon on the south side, me and Ben paused, sitting on our horses. A few moments later, gunfire filled the twilight with thunder. Curses and the sounds of breaking glass were heard. We watched the batwings of the saloon open. The man with the black frock coat and the red sash stalked out and continued marching toward's the Marshall's office. Moments later, men poured from the saloon.

"That's Wild Bill Hickock! He just gunned down Phil Coe and his two pards. I'm gonna check my gun's pronto!" Suddenly there was a rush up the street toward the Marshall's office. Ben swore.

"Five dead men in less than an hour, Abilene's a hell town, but that Hickock's gonna make her tame down in a hurry. C'mon, Kid, I don't like the smell of blood!" We rode for camp.

10

~ <u>MASSACRE</u> ~

*I*t wasn't long until we rode up before the fire at camp.

"Evenin' Cookie, how's grub?"

"Dad blast it! Jest once I'd like to hear sum'n else, 'cept, how's grub, er, whats fer breakfast? C'aint somebody, think of anything but eatin' 'round here?" I could see that Cookie was his old, cheerful self tonight.

"Sorry Cookie. Have you seen Red John?"

"Seen him? I wish I'd never laid eyes on him. He come staggerin' in here 'bout an hour ago huntin' you, kid. He tripped and fell right in my cobbler face first. Ruined it, thet's what he did! He's layin' over thar under the tarp, drunker'n Saturday night! Can't ya hear 'em snorin'?" I laughed. Strolling over, I looked down on Red John McDonald himself. His beard stuck up and it quivered when he snored.

Well, I had to go, and I guess that it was better that John was all passed out. I wanted him to be heading back to Texas with Ben rather than chasing after me, which is what he probably would want to do if he was sober. I wrote him a note asking him again to look after Ma and Jori Lee for me 'till I got home. I didn't plan on staying away for much more than a few more months. I knew that I had to face the music sooner or later.

"Bye John," I muttered. "Look after my folks real good, 'cause they're worth it!" All John did was give me an extra loud snore for an answer. After saying goodbye to Ben, I rode out under a full moon and a cloudless sky.

A little ways away I pulled up in the darkness and listened. I didn't hear anything but the lonesome wail of a coyote hunting his mate. The moon was big and yellow, a lover's moon, Jori used to say. Something was wrong, tho, with the night and I wondered what it was until I thought of the coyote and his lonesome wails. It was almighty lonesome sounding. It didn't help me none that I was mighty lonesome myself. So lonesome it hurt, even tho I had been with the other men in camp for over a year, this was a different lonesome.

Pa always said that animals could read your mind. He said that was the way that they communicated to each other. He must have been right, 'cause Diablo turned his head to look back at me, and then whickered softly nuzzling my leg. Funny, I didn't feel so lonesome anymore. I had my horse, and that was almost like having Pa around. Me and Pa had a lot in common, 'cause we both rode the Owl Hoot Trail and sometimes I could feel his presence just as if he was lookin' down on me, watchin' and smiling that slow, easy smile of his.

"Thanks Pa," I breathed, for makin' me a man!

Several days later I was deep in injun country. I rode slowly, enjoying the scenery.

"Magnificent, colossal, it was!" Jori Lee had a habit of using those two words to describe anything that she thought was grand. Well, them words couldn't begin to describe this country. The air was clean and fresh, and the senses were magnified until a man's head seemed to vibrate with pleasure. I had an urge to shout and my heart was filled to bursting with the grandeur of it all.

The plains rolled away, mile upon mile of waving yellow buffalo grass. Sage and hokecherry mixed with the prairie flowers of red, yellow and blue. Far in the distance, a purple haze hung over dark mountain buttresses. As I rode, the ground became more rolling, and arroyose. Boulders dotted the landscape. The wind ruffled the horse's manes and meadowlarks sang their liquid notes. Round depressions filled with dust marked the ancient Buffalo wallows. Lodge pole pines pierced great, white, thunderhead clouds and silhouetted themselves starkly against the deep blue sky.

The vastness of the land dwarfed me and my animals. Prairie falcons slid up and down the air drafts. I watched as one plummeted swiftly to earth. There was a shriek, and the bird with its prey lifted away to some secret nest on the mountain crest. The reality of death sobered me, and reminded me that only the strong survive in the wilderness.

It was nearing sundown. Darkness came sudden in this country and I'd have to camp soon. Again I heard a coyote singing its mournful song as I topped a small hill and looked down into the hollar below. I sat there in the saddle staring at the burned remains of three wagons! Death has a strong odor, and the stink was unmistakable. One body hung head down from a wagon wheel. The still-warm ashes of a fire glowed inches below his head.

Dismouning, I tethered the horses and walked closer. I counted seven bodies scattered in the scorched grass. The mules still lay in their harness, looking like huge pincushions. Their bodies were bloated and the stench of death hung everywhere. I turned away from the sight, bile rising in my throat.

The wagon that had been filled with buffalo hides was now just a pile of smoking ashes, singed hair and steel rims. The mutilated bodies were grizzly reminders of the red man's hatred for buffalo hunters. The injuns held the buffalo sacred. He was their food. He was their shelter and their medicine. When the white man began to kill the buffalo wholesale, he threatened the Indian's very existence. The Indian killed for food, but the white man killed for the money that the hides would bring in Dodge City, Kansas.

Now, I was feeling uneasy. My back tingled and I half expected an arrow to strike right between my shoulder blades.

"You fool, if you hang around here you're just asking for it! Them injuns and maybe even white renegades could be layin' up there in the rocks right now." I cursed myself for a fool I'd ridden right up just like a tender foot greenhorn. *'Red John sure wouldn't approve of your actions, boy. He'd snort disqustedly and say, Jest like a danged tenderfoot, go buttin' into somthin' what aint none of his business and git his fool head blowed off!'*

From now on, I had me a feeling that I ought to lay up durin' the day, and do my traveling at night. Red John's teaching renewed themselves in my mind as I looked around warily.

"Boy ya gotta hide yore tracks on hard pan rock, ride in streams, and stay away from the open. When ya come to a ridge, git off yer hoss an' sneak an' crawl up to the top. Then ye jest sneak a peek to see what's on the other side."

"Watch close for sign an' smoke, and pay attention to the animals. See if they're actin' natural. If birds fly, notice to see if somethin' skeered em'. Watch yer hoss's ears. He'll see, hear or smell anything before you do. Sticks and mud comin' downstream mean someone or something is above you. Hide and watch. Wear moccasins in injun territory. Keep your eyes peeled and don't make no fires or noise. Set snares fer yer meat and take 'em down when your through usin' em.''

"Put rawhide on your horse's feet for quiet on th' trail. Walk backwards where ya' can't help but have tracks. Dust yore tracks out with a bush in sand or dirt. Walk logs, and moss and stones an' such, to hid yore tracks. When ye camp, bury your ashes and yer hoss's dung. Black your face with charcoal or black mud fer night fightin', 'course, I favor the mud meself. Charcoal has the smell of smoke and fire, and an injun might locate ye from th' smell."

"Keep yore guns clean an' yer knives sharp. Yer life jest might depend on 'em, and don't throw nuthin away fer all to see. Train yor animals to keep quiet when they smell another horse, an' to come when ye signal 'em. Hand signal fer day and whistle fer night. Learn tannin' an' how to make yer own clothes. Everything ye need is in the wilderness if'n ye jest know how to git it." Red John had gone on and on, teaching me about how to survive.

"Well, Red, old Pard, it's time I started bein' a mountain man," I said soberly. I turned back to the horses and that is when I noticed the way they were actin'. Their ears were up and pointing toward a small clump of brush an' boulders just beyond what was left of the wagon. I was in a fix. Whoever was in there had me dead to rights. I hadn't no chance to defend myself ever if I tried so I just acted casual and I sountered around till I was where I could drop down behind a medium sized boulder. The only trouble was, the boulder was on the other side of the clearing away from my horses.

I sat down on the rock first, and then I acted like I saw something on the ground that interested me. When I bent over to see, I just flopped flat on my belly and started crawlin' away from there, keepin the rock between me and the place where whoever it was, was hidin'. After I got out of sight, I circled around quick, comin' up behind 'em. My gun was out and ready for business. Easing around a small clump of bushes on my hands and knees, I stopped and took in the situation. After all the trouble I'd went to, I wasn't much better off now than I was when I was out in the open.

I could see a place where a body had lain in the grass right there before me. But they weren't there now. Right about then I really began to get worried. I could feel that itch between my shoulder blades again. Best thing was to sit right where I was.

The sound of leather on stone and I had the wind knocked clear out of me! There was the glimpse of leather fringes, just before an arm grabbed me around the neck. Throwing myself backwards, violently driving the man against the stone, there was a whoosh of air past my ear. I broke away from the choke hold he had on me. It wasn't a minute too soon, either, because the man lunged at me again and in his hand was a razor sharp bowie knife! He pulled up when I showed him the muzzle of my old Navy. She was cocked and ready for bear. If that man had been any the least smart, I would have had to shoot him.

"Drop it quick, mister!" I grunted savagely,. "Now!" For a moment there I thought that he wasn't gonna do it. He glared at me and then his eyes just sort of glazed over and he fell right on his face. I picked up the knife that he had dropped. Then I nudged him with one foot.

"Git up, mister! Mister?" I rolled him over on his back

real careful, just in case he was play actin'. It was then that I saw the marks. *'Snakebite! A snake must have got him right in the jugular from the looks of it, poor devil! He'd hidden from the injuns only to get snake bit whilst he was hiding.'*

"Of all the bad luck! Well, here's to ya, mister, ya died game and a fightin!" I hunted around until I found where he had lain hid from the redskins underneath a rock overhang. Sure enough, right beside the marks of his body was a big old rattler. That snake didn't have a head. The man had severed its head from its body with one blow of his knife. But the dirty work was done and it was too late. The poison had worked fast. It was a wonder that he had found the strength to jump me the way he had.

It was getting dark now but I wasn't hankering to spend the night in this place of blood. It ain't the dead people that you have to look out for. Still, no man in his right mind likes to sleep next to a corpse. Midnight found me far from there, where I made a cold camp.

11
~ THE SIOUX ~

*S*everal days later I found what I was looking for, a large cavern like rock that jutted up and out aways, creating a big room-like shelter. There was room for both me and the horses if I worked it right by dividing the cave off with stones where it turned a little to the right. I'd build my fireplace where the rock split and an opening through the roof showed blue sky.

Situated between the two rooms, the head would keep me and the horses warm for the coming winter. The best thing about the place was the way it was located. It was high up and away from the trails, well hidden from view. It was perfect. A cold mountain stream ran close by, and a good-sized, clopping meadow lay below with plenty of grass for the horses. I could put up hay.

Willow and quaking aspen rustled in the wind along the stream bed, and blue astors with columbines colored the landscape. Game was plentiful and I'd see ermine, mink and fox. If I didn't find any gold, I sould still have a good harvest of fur. Although I hated trapping as a business, I had to live and make enough to give me and Jori a start someplace else. I didn't have much time. I'd been gone a year and a half already, and I couldn't expect Jori Lee to wait on me forever. It was time to get to work. Winter would soon be a cold reality. It comes early here in these parts.

I built the chimney first, mixing clay and lime for the mortar. When I was done, the only opening in the roof was plugged. I added the partition, connecting it. She worked just fine. I was careful to use only the kinds of wood that gave off little smoke. When I was finished with the cave it was almost like a fort. I had put in pegs for hanging things on the wall, and made myself a cot of cedar poles.

So far, I had seen no sign of a red man, or white man for that matter. This was virgin country. All around there was tall lodge pole pine and craggy granite bluffs. Little grassy parks held elk and buffalo, deer and bear. I had steak with mushrooms, clear cold water to drink, and some of the prettiest scenery that I had ever seen. There were bee trees and soon I would gather the honey into wood containers that I made just for that purpose.

"Why a man couldn't ask for anything more," I said to myself. "I could live here like a King, if only…if only Jori was here with me!" I had to work harder, so far my gold hunting, hadn't paid off. I would go higher on the mountain tomorrow, and try a new stream. There was a chill in the air, and any day now a blizzard would come roaring down from the north. Only a few more days, and my career as a prospector would be over. I didn't dare stay away from home any longer. I had to go back in the spring, hopefully with gold, to clear my name and marry Jori Lee.

My fodder for the horses was all gathered and there was hay, willow and aspen tips aplenty. The next day was cold, but I had a full beard now and warm furs. I had made mittens, and knee length moccasins with the hair inside. They allowed me to pad along the game trails as silent as any injun. So far, the wilderness agreed with me. It gave me what I needed. All I had to do was work for it. Nature is unforgiving, but she's generous with her gifts.

I climbed high up where the snow stayed year round, the wind whistled and moaned through the rocky outcrops. Once I saw little specks of white on a granite ledge. The little specks moved. Mountain goats! Mush-ice froze on my mittens as I panned the small stream.

"Color!" There was no mistaking it. Tiny flecks of gold! But there wasn't very much of it. I worked all day and climbed back down to camp at nightfall exhausted. I was dead tired. That night a cougar screamed and panicked the horses. Having to get up to quiet them, Diablo made almost as much noise as the cougar screaming back at the big cat. Everything quieted back down after I went outside and drove it off. He didn't like the man-smell I guess.

The next day, I killed a buck and jerked the venison. For as long as I could, I kept panning the small stream hoping to hit it big. Then, one morning, I awoke to find snow on the ground. Great snowflakes danced and spun on their way to the ground. The wind was rising, winter was here. There'd be no more panning for gold. I had only two small bags of dust, a pitiful showing for a summer's work. Well, I'd just have to trap those furs, after all!

Today, I'd make snowshoes so I could walk over the drifts instead of sinking deep inside them. The temperature was far below zero by dark, and the snow changed to sleet that pelted against the stone walls of my shelter. By midnight, the wind had risen from a low mourn to a high wail. This was shaping up to be a blizzard. A real *'blue norther'*, as they were called here in the west. It's when the temperature could drop fifty to eighty in the short span of an hour or two. I was comfortable and warm in my cave, while great white mounds of snow piled around the opening.

I was lonely, though. I had been thinking about Jori Lee a lot lately. I missed Ma, too. I jumped when one of the trees popped outside. The extreme cold froze the sap and exploded the trees from the inside. Snow sifted in around the buffalo robes I had hung from the opening to the cave.

Three days later, the blizzard subsided, but the great cold remained. The snow crusted over and I heard a new sound, one that I had heard only once before. It lifted on the air rising higher, and then dying out beneath a cold, frozen moon.

"Wolves!" The horses whickered and stamped, nervous at hearing the pack's hunting cry. As the cold persisted, the game became scarce, until the wolves were forced to hunt constantly, to stay alive. The wolf is King in snow. It finds its prey not as agile in the deep snow and easier to run down. They began to sit outside my shelter, growling at the smell of meat. Gradually, they became bolder. I had found their tracks just outside the frozen buffalo robe over the opening and I didn't like it one bit.

The wolves were starving. They were trying to get at the horses, but there was no opening except through my door, and the man smell kept them back. They knew that I was inside. Finally, the leader of the pack, a huge gray beast, that must have weighed well over one hundred and fifty pounds, entered the opening, cautiously. His yellow-eyes staring and his tongue run out over long yellow fangs.

"Hi Grayface!" I laughed as the wolf jumped and growled fiercely. I could see the muzzles of two or three more thrust inside the robe covering. The horses were going crazy with fear. They stamped and whickered. The stallion screamed his challenge and warning to the wolves. I got up to replenish the fire, moving slowly, watching grayface to see what he would do. The great jaws opened and the lobo snarled. He began to stalk closer. I had no desire to kill the wolf, but this situation would not do at all. I picked up a stick from the wood pile, my hand on my colt for added assurance. Gray face was getting ready to rush me as I raised the stick and threw it.

The big wolf lowered his head and snarled at me just before the heavy chunk of firewood bounced off his shoulder. The snarl changed instantly to a yelp of painful surprise. Then the lobo was gone into the night. Moments later, I heard the pack's hunting cry in the distance. I wondered what unlucky animal was being hunted as I listened to the savage, cry.

I was up at daybreak feeding the horses. Today I would check my deadfalls. After breakfast, I mushed off down to the valley on the pair of snowshoes I had made out of green skin. The hide had shrunk on the frames of the snow-shoes as it dried, forming a tight, strong framework. It was some awkward on those contraptions, though. Every time I tried to go fast, I ended up sprawled in the snow. After about two or three times falling, I began to get the hang of it. You shuffled your feet instead of walking. Just about then I shuffled on a snag sticking up out of the snow. That time it hurt.

"Dang snowshoes, I'll never git used to 'em." I gritted my teeth and rubbed my hip.

"Boy," Pa used to say, "Complainin' never done nobody any good! Don't waste no energy on it. Just hang in there and try harder, an' ya'll git the job done!"

"Yes sir!" I mumbled to myself. "I'm gonna make it

work, Pa, no more complainin'!'"

There wasn't any fur in the dead falls. The animals could have moved down to the lower elevations, and the rest were hibernating deep under the snow. The wolves weren't the only ones that were having a hard time making a go of it. The provisions and jerky that I had put up for the winter, was getting pretty low. I had to find game if I could. I started moving less and looking more as I traveled the game trails at the lower end of the valley.

It was deathly quiet and still. The snow muffled my steps. Most people would do a lot better at hunting game if they would learn to see better in the woods. Pa always used to see game before I did, and I couldn't figure out how he did it until one day I got peeved at myself and asked him.

"Son, what are you looking for?" he asked me.

"Why, a deer." I answered.

"The whole deer?" He grinned then and I grinned back. Boy was I stupid. I had been looking for a deer alright, but I had expected to see the whole animal, big as life, right out in the open.

"First off, deer look smaller when they're in the woods, so look for something about the size of a dog. Look for an ear, a leg, or watch for movement. You never see the whole deer right off. When you see movement, boy, just freeze and focus your attention on the spot that moved. Eventually, you may get to see the deer before it see's you. Most times, if your waitin' to see the whole deer, it'll see you first and spook. You have to learn to see through trees and brush, and into the shadows where deer hide. When ya sit down to wait, sit in the shade. Ya kin always see into the sun from the shade, but you can't sit in the sun and see into the shade, remember that."

Pa went on teaching me.

"Skyline the deer instead of your self, deer like to travel the low ground, such as arroyos, gullies and the like. Pay attention to where the heaviest trails are and where they go. Study your game animal, and know what he eats, where he sleeps, and his everyday habits. Then, you got it made."

Pa was right, except for one thing, I couldn't see any tracks in the snow, and what do you do when the animals have all moved away? Still, most of the animals around here fed in the meadow by the stream, so I should have some luck there.

I cut over to the right and started edging along the brook. *'There!'* First movement, and then the tips of antlers showed themselves above the brush. The antlers were huge and heavy-beamed. I stood still, waiting. The elk moved and I could see his head and neck. I marveled at the size of the animal. The meat would be tough as old shoe leather. This must be the bull of the woods, around these parts. *'Well, I might as well just move on, nobody but wolves can eat pure gristle and rawhide, which is what this old bull shaped up to be.'* I grinned, picked me up a fistful of snow, shaped 'er up real good, and cut loose on old *'beller-er box.'* That was the best throw I had ever made. The snowball hit 'ol' beller', right, square in the brech-block. Either he spit out his cud that he was chewing on, or he swallered-it, I couldn't tell.

He was bucking up and down in one spot for a minute or two before his legs caught up with his intentions and he busted out o' there. I like to have died laughing. My laughing didn't last long. Seems that old bull had him a following of fat, juicy young cows and I watched, open-mouthed, as they bounded away through the pines. I took out after the whole bunch. I thought I might get a shot if the bull broke out into the open. I could still hear the elk as they ran crashing through the brush.

The snowshoes pulled at my feet, and I was breathing hard. Then even the noise was gone and I couldn't see nothin'. The last trace I seen of the group was the white rump patch of the old bull, disappearing into the pine timber. I stopped.

"Of all the fool tricks, that last one had been a humdinger!" The only game I had seen in days and I'd let foolish sentiment play me for a fool. "Kid tricks! Throwin' snowballs! Well, there was no use to cry over spilt milk." I checked the Winchester. There was no snow in the muzzle or the breech which Pa had taught me to do. Red told me that he seen a man git kilt that way once.

"Many a dang fool's went to his maker with a gun barrel ah' stickin' out o' his head jest 'cause he pulled the trigger with snow a' cloggin' the muzzle!"

I had taken another look around me and was some surprised to see a wolf slippin' along through the timber. Then came another and another, and began to bunch up. They stopped, and were focusing on something by the edge of the pines. Then they began to circle and I knew that they had something cornered over there. The circle began to tighten as I took out toward them. I could hear their snarles and I knew that I'd have to be real careful or I might be included in their plans for supper.

Wolves will fight for their kill, even if it's against a mountain lion or a bear. I grinned to myself, things were certainly looking better, maybe that was a young deer that the pack had cornered over there. I was close enough to see the wolve's breath as they panted and snarled. Then I heard the cry. It sounded almost human! I stopped, and tried to see what made the sound. Then a thin, emaciated figure rose weakly to its feet before the pack. Feebly waving a stick, the slight figure tried to strike out at the wolves. I stared at the ragged apparition. It was a human being! For a moment, I was so shocked that I couldn't move.

The pack rushed in and I saw the creature go down before the lobo's attack! I had to do something quick! I raised the Winchester and fired a shot directly over the backs of the wolves as I feared that I might hit the man if I shot at them directly. A couple of them broke away, yelping. I must have clipped them. I emptied the '73 watching snow explode under the wolves' feet as they ran. I watched the pack ghost away through the timber, disappearing quickly from sight, all except for one. That one looked back over his shoulder then raised his muzzle to the sky and howled. It was Gray Face! He howled his anguish at being robbed of his dinner. His high head dropped, to stare at me and growl, he turned and was gone. I ran forward and dropped to my knees before an old injun! Kneeling, I lifted the old man's head and the eyes fluttered open.

"Hey Aaah!" The bony arms lashed out and got me square on the nose, bringing tears to my eyes.

"Hold on old timer! I'm friendly! Ow! Cut it out now! Friend, see? Meee friend!" I smiled and pointed to myself, being careful to stay back out of reach. The thin arms continued to flail. The old man passed out. I could go closer to him. I felt of my bleeding nose.

"Dang it, chief, we gotta smoke the peace pipe, so's I kin git you back to camp!" After examining him, I decided that the wolves had not hurt him badly. His buckskins were torn up and exposure had taken its toll of the old man's strength. He was well-nigh frozen too! I cut two stout poles for a travois.

Mor'n likely the shootin;' would bring more red skin's down around my neck, but I had to help.

"Confound it, chief, what are you doing out here anyway? Where's your people? Sentimental fool, that's what I was. I'd be willing to bet, just as soon as the ol' coot's people show up, I'd be scalped. The old man would probably holler louder than the rest. Yep, if'n I kept on acting the way I was, I was gonna go under from pure dumb, if'n I didn't starve first. Now I had me another mouth to feed, and meat was gettin's scarce.

I searched for more injun sign but the only tracks visible were the old' man's, the wolves and mine.

"Time to go, old man, are you still on the warpath?" His faded eyes stared unseeingly, then, the old Indian began to chant hoarsely.

"Haii-eeee-ohhhh-oh! Haneaaah 'o! Haneeeeh naaaanaaa nooooh!" Then he cried out in a broken but still defiant voice, "Hopo! Hoka Hey!" *'That's Sioux talk.'* I stared apprehensively, *'and the Sioux are on the warpath!'*

The words meant roughly, "C'mon, let's go! The same thing as 'Charge', to a Calvary patrol. The old brave was still thrashing around while I tied him to the travois. Lifting the poles to my shoulders, I looked down.

"Well, time to go, chief." The old Indian struck down imaginary enemies, shooting arrows, and counting coup. I grinned at him deciding that he had been a tough warrior in his day, for shore! He went on stabbing, slashing, and clubbing feverishly.

"Yeah, Chief, I'd hate to have had you fer an enemy when you were younger, I bet you got scalps ah plenty. Ya probably gave all the squaws fits, too!" I couldn't help but chuckle at the thought. The old injun got still then and he grinned wolfishly.

"Ho, Ha, Heh, white man," he grunted, which meant in Sioux for 'Go in Peace'. "Hopa, hokahey."

By the time I got that old man back to camp, I was all tuckered out and winded. It was snowing again, and the sky was a gray lead color. It felt like I had a dozen blisters from the snowshoes. Staggerin' around the cave, I stoked up the fire and heated up some hot water. I bathed the chief's chest and face.

"Whew!" I whistled. "The old buzzard had enough knife an' arrow scars to cover a buffalo hide." I felt two ridged scars on the old injun's chest.

"Sundance!" I knew what those scars meant. Red John had explained to me about the ritual. It required great pain and courage. Skewers of bone were thrust through the chest muscles. Then rawhide thongs were looped over the skewers and tied to a central pole in a circle. There were other Indians dancing attached to the pole. They all danced in to touch the pole and then backwards to the thong ends, pulling and jerking backwards.

The object was to tear free from the skewers by ripping the flesh from the body. If a dancer passed out from the pain, he was disqualified and held in disgrace. Once the dance had begun, the only honorable way out was to tear free no matter how long it took. Still few were strong enough to complete the game. Only the strongest and very brave would endure till their skin finally tore

"An' they'll be a few more scars from the wolf bites!" I dressed the old man's wounds and bandaged them tightly. The wounds didn't worry me none, it was the fever. If'n it wasn't pneumonia, he was awful close to it. The injun was in a bad way. His breathing was labored and ragged. Mebbe I could pull him through mebbe not. Could be both of us would go under if the snow didn't let up. I had to have some game and soon.

"Might have to eat the packhorse," I thought miserably.

"Games moved on down to the lower parts where it's warmer, and the snow's not so deep. I'd just have to follow 'em." I raised my head and listened. The wind was rising, an' it was some colder.

"Well, at least we were snug and warm. I had to heat the old man up slowly. Too quick could kill him! What was he doin' out there all by his lonesome?" I gnawed at the problem like a dog with a bone. Sometimes the old people were cast out of their Indian camp to die, but this one didn't look to be that old, now that I had looked him over more carefully. If he wasn't half-froze and sick, he'd be in his forties, I guessed. He was still able-bodied, and a tribe needed all the men it could get!

Still puzzled, I fed the old Chief hot broth. He had no weapons of any kind, not even a knife. I'd made sure of that, nothing but the skins on his back. The old man was game, I had to give him that much. His feet and hands were frostbitten, but he'd still tried to fight the wolves! He was a Sioux, there was no doubt in my mind. 'Course the words 'white man', had been English. Mighty few Indians speak English. Those that could were either scouts for the army or maybe some of the higher chiefs. Well there was no use to worry about it, it was time to get some shut eye. I had to find game tomorrow or else!

The next day I was up before full light, melting snow for the horses. Ice crystals floated in the air and there was a crust on the snow thick enough to walk on. It was some thick, though. I gave the horses their ration of willow tips and dried grass. The old man was resting easy, still sleeping although his fever was still high. I hated to leave him, but I had no choice. We had to eat. I wrapped my knee moccasins with twisted rawhide thongs. Maybe it would give me a little more traction on the crust. The blisters were still painful and smarted considerably.

Moving slowly because of my sore feet, I taken off down toward the valley. After walking a while, my feet quit bothering me so much, and I moved a little easier.

"Blisters busted!" I mumbled to myself. The air was too cold to breath. I had to take in a little at a time to keep from freezing my lungs. The wind whipped the red wool cloth I had wrapped around my face. Then ragged long johns, shore come in handy, mighty handy! I had walked for the better part of an hour with the wind in my face. Any hunter who knows anything hunts into the wind. I stopped to rest, breathing real carefully.

The snow seemed to be over and the sun shone gold against the snowy pine tops. The granit crags of the mountains rose high up into the blue sky. I had blacked my cheekbones to keep from getting snow blindness. I would have been blinded by now if I hadn't. I was starting to move on when I saw the tracks. Deep and splay-footed, they led into the timber.

"Old Beller!" I began to follow them. They passed through deep thickets where the light was dim, continuing on to emerge on the edge of the meadow. Straight across, the great tracks disappeared into the pines beyond. I crossed, and then as I started to enter the thicket on the other side, I was pulled up short by a deep, angry bellow! That's when I saw my first flying wolf! The lobo's body came sailing up and out of that pine thicket to land in front of me. The wolf's back was broken!

Whimpering, it tried to crawl away. Then the old elk come crashing out of the woods, shakin' his head and stompin' his hooves. That elk shore was livin' up to the name I give him! He'd beller and charge those wolves and they were havin' a tough time of it staying out of his way.

He nearly got another one of them. Slipping and sliding, the wolves couldn't seem to keep their footing on the icy crust. The pack must have been desperate, to take on a tough, old, king elk like him. Boy, he was somethin', that old bull, ah blowin' with his nostrils all red, his eyes full of fire and fright.

He was winning until fate stepped in and dealt him a losing hand. The thick crust broke through under his heavy weight, his hindquarters sinking deep into a drift. He'd made a fatal mistake and should have stayed off the deep drift by the stream but it was too late now. He heaved and lunged, but the more he struggled, the deeper he got, ending up sitting on his backside just like a man in his easy chair.

At that moment, I could have sworn that ol' Grayface, the king wolf, grinned! His tongue hung out over his big, yellow fangs as he looked at that old bull elk. Seemed I could almost read his mind. I imagined he'd be sayin' to his foe,

"Ya fit ah good fight, but we gotcha now, pard!" One of the lobos would cut in and that ol' bull elk would raise his front hooves and strike out just like a man! He was still full of fight and had plenty of sand! When the wolves saw that he was trapped, they started to close in, and this time, they'd finish him. I just couldn't let em git ol' Beller! I ran straight at the pack, yellin' as loud as I could. I slipped on the crust and fell, pulling myself up and stumbling. This time old Grayface and his bunch wasn't havin' none of it. They turned quick and throwed a circle around one Rance Rainey! I put the brakes on fast!

"Whoa now, Grayface! GIT!" The wolf's hackles were up along with his temper and he was mad! I stared straight down that red throat and saw the killing light in his eyes.

I'd pushed the pack too far. Their snarls got meaner and more savage. I threw up my '73 but before I could pull the trigger, I noticed the snow halfway up the barrel!

The fall, the muzzle was clogged with ice and snow. If I pulled the trigger, the gun would blow up in my face. There just wasn't time to go for my colt under the buffalo coat I wore! Saliva dripped from Grayface's jaws. The wolf was only ten feet away. I knew I couldn't but I had to try anyway. I grabbed at the .44, and the movement triggered Grayface to rush. I saw a shadow like a bird flit across the snow and hit Grayface, *'Kerr thunk!'* The wolf was on me in that split second, and I went down. The crushing weight of the big wolf was pressing me deeper into the snow.His teeth tore at my thick coat. He had my arm in his jaws and if it hadn't have been for the buffalo coat, I'd have lost that arm!

A moment later, I was out from under him. Grayface lay full-length in the snow at my feet. A red stain grew in the snow around the big animal. A feathered shaft quivered in the wolf's side as he breathed heavy, labored gasps. His warm breath from his lungs was visible escaping into the cold air from his wound. His last breath was a struggle, and there was no more. As he lay still, a startling sound caused me to jump near out of my coat and britches.

"Haiieeee, Yiee, Yieee!" The Sioux's cry echoed between the hills, sending the rest of the wolves racing away. I was mighty disgusted with myself. I'd been a goner that time, for sure! I watched a young Indian run lightly up to where I was standing. I kept my colt handy just in case.

"How! Koda, White-eyes!" I was hoping that he was saying hello in a friendly way. The Indians eyes were black and somewhat slanted, his cheekbones prominent in a face that had a certain foxy look. I decided right then and there that he would do to keep an eye on. Tryin' to be civil, I mumbled,

"Lo, Injun!" The redskin then started to rub it in by asking me,

"You mebbee lose horse, white-eyes? You gonna ride old wapiti? He make big strong mount, see? He sits in snow for you to climb on back!" That dratted redskin was grinnin' from ear to ear! I was still tryin' to think of something to say when he opened up again.

"Why you no speak? Mebbee you see poor injun's arrow? Is very poor arrow, shoot crooked. Injun think mebbee him come this way?" Yep, just as I had figured before, most injuns couldn't speak English, but them that could, was all smart alecks! I noticed that the buck had another arrow necked and ready. *'Take it easy'*, I told myself. *'He might be a wise-crackin, smart aleck, redskin, but he shore saved my bacon!'* I spat to clear my throat.

"O.K., Injun, ya had your fun and I guess I deserve a little razzin. I'm shore beholdin' to ya fer the way ya done ol' Grayface in. I was fixin to be his supper!" I stuck my hand out to shake. The indian's grin vanished. For a minute there I thought that he was gonna have at me with that bow and arrow. His black eyes narrowed. Then after a moment, the injun turned and bent over the lobo.

"Haiieeee! Here arrow! Wolf find! Him make nice pelt, too! Go good with white-eye's scalp!" The injun grinned again.

"Hold it now, Injun, ya wouldn't be meanin' my scalp now, would ya?" I was commincin' to get riled. "If you are, have at it then, redskin!" I said cockin' Pa's Navy colt.

"No hurry, injun wait, mebbee you good man? Not bad like other white-eyes. Him shakes hands with injun, twist arm, throw poor injun horse trough. White-eyes laugh at injun. His friends laugh. Him heap bad man. Injun no like bad white-eyes, injun kill!" The brave's eyes burned and he stroked a scalp dangling from his knife sheath. The scalp was red and curly. It didn't take no dim wit to figure out that, either the bad white-eyes was dead, or he was runnin' around without his scalp. The buck cocked his head. "But, mebbee you good man, eh? Come, we get old wapiti out of hole."

Both of us slid poles under that old elk's front hooves to give him traction and watched him pull himself out of the hole. We had to run real quick-like when ol Beller-box come outa there pawin' and buglin'! Wapiti, or whatever the injun called him, wasn't grateful none, for what we had done for him. I thought we was gonna have to shoot him. Finally though, after he pawed and tossed them big ivory tines o'his, he took out of there for the high timber.

"I still ain't got no meat," I grumbled. Seems like, all my luck was bad all of a sudden. Now, I had me two redskins to worry about. The injun buck spoke up again.

"White-eyes need meat? Me have nice, young buck in tree. We go get, sure. Injun heap big hunter. White-eyes mebbee cook? Him bad hunter, him be cook. Squaws work, hey?" I eyed him narrowly. This could get right tiresome, takin' lip from a no-account, smart-aleck injun buck. He wasn't much mor'n a kid, at that!

"Ok, I git your drift redskin, now, what's your name and tribe? Seems to me it's mighty cold to be out huntin', lessin ya need meat bad. Is your tribe gettin' low on meat, maybe?"

"Me Sioux tribe, tribe all time need meat. Me no hunt meat, me look for grandfather. Me called Tashunka Witko!" So the kid was looking for his grandfather, huh, maybe I could have the last laugh, after all.

"Grandfather, eh? Just what might his name be, injun?" The brave looked at me steadily. "Him called Red Cloud." I choked,

"R-Red Cloud, that Sioux fire brand?" Oh lordy, was I ever running in bad luck. "An, what does Tash-Tusk-er, what does your name mean in English?" I closed one eye and glared, trying to act unimpressed before this upstart of an injun kid.

"Me Crazy Horse!" said the young Indian. Hell, fire, and brimstone! I felt my hair prickle. I looked around for the war party I was sure would come ki-yi-yi-ing over the snow to collect my scalp. Crazy Horse was real calm about it all.

"No worry, white-eyes, me think mebbee you good man!"He said solemnly."

"I'm glad", I breathed. "I'm everlastingly soo glad, Injun. Now, let's git that meat o' your'n and hit th' trail back to my camp. I think I gotta big surprise fer you."

I watched the old Chief by the fire. It sure was hard to believe that the old man was the fierce war Chief of the whole Sioux nation, Ogallallah, Bad Face, Sioux at that. Crazy horse had set right in to doctorin' the old coot. He fixed poultices, and made big medicine as I watched silently. I had me a hunch it wasn't no time to be disturbin' the ceremonies.

That Crazy Horse shore set a lot o' store by his uncle. Grandfather was only a term of respect injuns paid to their elders. 'Course the Chief hadn't looked so old after his buckskins were off. Although his face was seamed and wrinkled, his body was well developed and strong. The slightness had been deceiving. Starvation and exposure had weakened and falsly aged the Chief. He was a mighty tough old bird. I doubted if a whiteman would have made it.

I shook myself out of my day dreams. Speaking of a

white man making it, Mr. Rainey, ya better start into thinkin' about how you're gonna git out of this scrape without being scalped. There was only one answer to my problem. Make a run for it, and do it while crazy horse was doctorin' the Chief. Only trouble was, the chances were a might slim that I could make it. I had ridden in here to strange country and I still didn't know that much about it. Them redskins was born here and they knew every trail, rock and bush through these black hills. Yeah, I had about as much a chance of making it out of here as a snowball in the devil's playground.

Of course, the only injuns that knowed I was here was Crazy Horse and his uncle. The worn, polished grip of the old Navy felt cool under my hand. *'No!'* Crazy fool that I was! I couldn't shoot down a man that had saved my life! *'Red John, old pard,'* I groaned, *'Your teachin' was all fer nothin. This ol' boy's gonna git killed 'cause o' them fool sentiments ya wuz always rantin' and snortin' about.'*

"Honorable?" Red John would grimace, "Honorable dead ya mean! Survival, boy, that's what it's all about. Ye gotta survive. Fight! An' survive! They h'aint nuthin else that matters none! Then Red John's face faded away in my mind and Pa Rainey's face took its place. Through the sea of confusion that clouded my brain I could hear his voice, slow and steady.

"Son, a man's got to have respect for himself. If'n he doesn't have that, anything else he gets, he'll never enjoy it. He'll always know he cheated, and nothin' belongs to him. Ya gotta have respect, son, so ride the honor trail, come what may!"

'Thanks, Pa. I'll never make ya ashamed, I promise! I looked at the two injuns by the fire. Come mornin', I'd ride out, injuns or no injuns. I was a free man. Only trouble was, Crazy Horse might not cotton to the idea. I'd handle that problem when it come. I rolled up in my skins and it was a long time before I fell asleep.

I was haunted by a slim, blue-eyed girl back in Texas. A girl, that likely I'd never see again. *Blasted Rock! Feels like its as big as a mountain!* I turned over, rubbing my eyes, and looked straight into the coal black eyes of Red Cloud. He grunted,

"Hah! White-eyes make loud noise in sleep! Him sound like grizzly bear!" I stared in consternation. *Why in dad blame, tarnation didn't I leave him there in the snow?* I groaned. It was clear where that nephew of his got his big mouth! Now I had me two healthy injuns on my hands, and time was a'wastin'! I rolled out of my bed roll and reached for my Winchester. It wasn't there! It was gone! No, it wasn't gone, it was right there in the hands of Red Cloud! That pesky uncle or grandfather, or whatever relation to Crazy Horse he was supposed to be, was sittin' there next to the fire just as bold as brass, admiring my rifle! Raising the '73, he sighted along the barrel.

"Good rifle, white man, him shoot fast?"

"Yeah?" I grunted, put out. "Him shoot fast." Well, I still had my .44 and my Spencer. I rolled my skins and started packin' up to leave. I grabbed a parflech of jerky. It would have to do, there was no time for more. At any minute, thousands of painted redskins were gonna pour down into the valley and I'd be trapped here in the cave.

The Sioux nation was made up of many different tribes. There was the Ogallalla, the Minniconjiou, the Hunkapapa, like old Sittin' Bull, the Sans Arc, and several more. Like I said, Sittin' Bull was medicine man of the great Hunkapapa tribe, which numbered in the hundreds all by itself. The Southern Cheyenne was the Sioux's cousins, which added a few thousand more injuns. And then there was the Northern Cheyenne…

'O' Lordy, Pa, I hope your stickin' with me today, 'cause I'm gonna need some help, for shore.' The Cheyenne backed up the Sioux, and the Sioux backed up the Cheyenne. Thousands of wild, painted redskins and I was right smack in the middle of them! I was settin' in a cave with the same injun who had told the US of A government to get out of the black hills! This was the man who had burned Forts to the ground. The very same *RED CLOUD!'*

I fed and watered the horses, and then I saddled them as fast as I could. Red Cloud watched impressively, but his eyes hid amusement. The white man was in a hurry to leave and he acted a little scared. He was also angry at something and Red Cloud believed that he knew what it was. All the time I was getting ready, I kept my eyes on that old buzzard. When I was set, I started to lead the horses outside. I ran smack into Crazy Horse, and he was carrying my Spencer!

"Good! You wake! Bring Horses, We go now, Friends come!" I groaned. *'That tears it, Rainey, ya fool, git ready to die! No chance now to make a run for it!'*

I was tempted to try anyway, 'till I seen old Red Cloud's face. He was watching me with that slant-eyed look wolves got when they're tryin' to slash your throat. He was watchin' close, and the Winchester pointed in my direction steady and true. I heard horses and in a moment more the cave was full of mean-eyed, Sioux!

A heavy-set, powerful brave spoke hoarsely to Crazy Horse. Crazy Horse answered in the Sioux dialect. Again, the brave spoke to Crazy Horse vehemently, glaring at me and waving his arms. The man lunged toward me, pulling a wicked- looking knife!

12
~ <u>THE HATRED OF GALL</u> ~

I did about the fastest draw in my life right then, but I held fire. It was a good thing that I did, because Crazy Horse jumped in front of the other brave and blocked him with the Spencer. They argued some more, then Crazy Horse made a chopping motion downward with this hand which seemed to be a sign for 'enough, the talk is over.' The mean one scowled, and stalked from the cave.

"Whew!" I breathed, after the other braves had followed the mean one out of the cave. "What was that all about?"

"Him ask why prisoner still have guns. Me say you no prisoner, you friend. Him say no white man friend to injun. Him want kill you quick."

"Yeah, I noticed that he wasn't overly friendly." I said sarcastically. "What's his name?"

"You watch good, him hate white-eyes much. Him called Pizi by tribe. Name mean bitter, like poison. Him kill many enemies, great warrior!" There was respect in Crazy Horse's tone of voice.

Later on, I kept my eyes on the one called Pizi and I

noticed that none of the other braves crowded him. He was what some would call handsome, very muscular, and well-built. I was soon to know that the brave's name was well branded. Pizi, the bitter one, was full of hatred of the white man! There was another thing that Crazy Horse told me. The man's name in English was "Gall!"

Old Red Cloud was the hero, I noticed. When we camped that night he stood by the fire and gave a big speech in the Sioux language. There was a lot of ki-yi-ying and haw-hawing at his big medicine. He made a motion with his hand and before I could say anything, two of his braves grabbed my arms and stood me up beside the war Chief! Red Cloud put his hand on my shoulders and said something real slow and solemn. All of the other injuns stood up when he did this. All but one! Pizi scowled darkly and turned his back to all of us.

"Grandfather, thanks you for taking him into your camp." Crazy horse stated simply. "You are welcome as a friend by our people" Pizi grumbled disgustingly and stalked off into the night. Crazy Horse's eyes followed Pizi. "There are those among us that are not your friend, White-eyes, watch well!" I kept my eyes turned away from the fire. I nodded, for the light made a man half blind in darkness.

"Never look into the fire, son," Pa told me, so I rolled my blankets well away from the fire, out of the light. Then after I figured everyone was asleep, I got up and moved to another place. I taken the Russian .44 to bed with me and I lay there wide awake, listening. Along up toward morning I heard the soft swish of leather in the grass off to the side of the camp. Someone was moving around out there, real quiet-like. I lay still, but I got ready to roll and come up shootin'! The form of an injun rose up from the grass and I could see his outline clearly against the night sky. Laying still, as if I was lost in deep sleep, watching, waiting, it was a long time before the shadow moved again.

Whoever, it was moved real careful toward me. Another form rose up from the ground off to my left. This one had a rifle and I heard the loud sound of its action as it was cocked. The shadows moved together. I could hear their whispered conversation between them. The larger of the two moved away, then back the way he had come. The smaller shadow eased back to the ground. I turned over and let the hammer back down on the Russian, smiled and went on to sleep.

In the darkness close by, a slim young Sioux brave watched closely. He heard the white man turn over and the hammer of his gun click. Crazy Horse smiled with grim humor. It appeared that the old grandfather had been unduly worried over his new white friend. This white man was not soft and lazy like most of the whites Crazy Horse had known. This one could take care of himself.

"Sleep well, white-eyes," he spoke respectfully. There was no answer. The white man was asleep. The young brave grinned again. It had not been the white man's life Crazy Horse had saved this night. The life had been that of Pizi's!

It was a big village. The lodges were smoke blackened and the cooking fires sent smoke pouring up and out of the smoke flaps. Dogs barked and children squealed, playing the games of 'snow snake,' and roll the hoop. The village was set up by a small stream in a big meadow. Our horses were taken by two injun boys. The boys were trying awful hard to look grown up and important. The smallest one was standing on tiptoe, trying to match the height of his companion. I grinned,

"I reckon kids are the same everywhere." Crazy Horse

handed the reins of his pony to the smallest boy.

"Care for my friend's horses well!" he commanded, giving the boys a proud, haughty look. Diablo rolled his eyes and pranced, flattening his ears, showing his big yellow teeth wildly.

"Aieee! Devil horse!" the boys looked at the big horse with awe. Half-frightened, the biggest boy gently grasped the stallion's reins and lead the horses away, staying carefully out of reach of the big stallion's teeth.

"You sure they can handle him?" I looked at CrazyHorse. He waved his hand.

"All Sioux boys know how to handle horse very young. Soon, make friend with spotted stallion. Come, we eat!"

I followed Crazy Horse into the lodge that smelled of smoke and sage. An old squaw sat by the fire, chewing on a wolfskin.

"She eatin' that?" I asked Crazy horse open-mouthed. The brave grinned.

"No, old grandmother chew on skin to make soft. Women's work." He grunted at the old squaw and she got up and went to the fire. In just a few moments she dipped out two steaming helpings of a type of venison stew.

I was hungrier than I thought. After eating all of our helpings, Crazy Horse licked his fingers and belched loudly. He started to stare at me real mean-like. I finally realized what was wrong. To an Indian, belching after a meal is proper manners. If you don't belch, then it figures that you didn't like the meal, and that is a direct insult to the host. I leaned backwards and belched as loud as I could, rubbing my stomach. Crazy Horse smiled then, satisfied. He pulled out a pipe and we proceeded to smoke it. The smoke was strong and acrid. It burned my throat. I wasn't used to smokin' but I'd soon get the habit of it if I stayed around these injuns for very long. Seems like everything they did had to be smoked over, celebrated, or meditated about.

"Grandfather call big council tonight. Whole tribe be there. Big Medicine!" Crazy Horse spread his arms. "Hunkpappa's come. Many squaws," he grinned. An' I swear, the black eyes of that injun was plumb full of devilment. "Mebbee Red Cloud buy wife for white friend. Hunkpapa squaws big and fat, keep white man warm in winter!"

I got up and walked outside the lodge, watching the injun kids playing 'snow snake'. One kid would roll a hoop of willow across the packed snow and ice, then another took a stick shaped like a sled runner with the tip bent up and he would slide this 'snow snake' across the snow and through the hoop. When I started to move on, I noticed that Crazy Horse was stickin' real close, along with one of his friends, Spotted Elk. I figured then, that I just wasn't really trusted yet by these redskins. I can't say I blamed them. The white man had given most injuns nothing but grief. I noticed that winter was dealing with these particular injuns pretty hard.

Blizzards that lasted for days cut down the Sioux's food, supplies, and hunger was a deep, gnawing pain in the belly. Sickness came at these times, mostly to the old people and the children. Many of them died. Hunting was impossible until the blizzards blew themselves out. They lived on roots and plants, too, but these were frozen deep under the snow. If it hadn't been for the camp dogs, times would have been a lot harder for Red Cloud's people.

Now, I got nothin' against dogs in general. But after I seen my first dog get cooked, I found it mighty hard to partake of camp cookin' after that. Me and Crazy Horse was settin' in at a bone game with Spotted Elk and Hump,

a Hunkpapa, when a squaw come stormin' out of her lodge
with a big stick in her hand. Crazy Horse and the rest of
them bucks looked at each other and grinned, slappin' and
jabberin' amongst themselves, pointing at the old squaw.
Crazy Horse turned to me.

"You watch, White-Eyes, heap fun mebbee." Well, that
ol' squaw commenced to eye some of the camp dogs ah
layin' around camp, finally, settling her gaze on a slim, little
yellow dog that was just mindin' his own business. That
little ol' dog seen her lookin' and he knew that old squaw
was up to no good. He started to edge away from there.
The old Squaw taken out after him, but she missed, he had
dodged between her legs. She hit the ground and come up
screaming just as mad as could be. She ran that little yeller
dog all over camp, slippin' and slidin', screamin' and fallin'!
She shore was having a devil's time of it, tryin' to put meat
on the table. Before long the whole camp was in an uproar.

People who say injuns don't laugh should'a seen that
show down. Injuns were rollin' on th' ground, laughin' and
hootin', holding their sides. Crazy Horse and his boys
slapped their legs and teased the old squaw mercilessly. It
didn't make no never mind how the squaw begged and
pleaded for help, there just wasn't no takers. It was too
much fun watchin' that little yellow dog make a plumb fool
out of her.

That little dog looked like he was enjoyin' it, too! With
his tongue hangin' out, he looked like he was laughin! It
being late winter, most of the slow dogs had already hit the
pot. That left all the young, fast ones, and that little dog
was the fastest. He dodged around speedier than a jack
rabbit. Finally, that ol' squaw just set down an' gave up,
tryin' to catch her breath. That little dog had won!

The braves were still teasin' the squaw when I heard the

bow twang and seen the little dog fall to the ground with a yelp of pain. It got awful quiet for a while. Whimpering, the dog tried to get up, but the arrow pinned both his hind legs together. Pizi pulled out the arrow, causing the dog to yelp again.

"There, Grandmother, now you can catch your meat," he growled. Mercy is not in the Indian's list of desirable traits, but respect for courage and prowess in battle is. What Pizi had done was not accepted as good sportsmanship. There was a low murmur of disapproval among the Indians looking on. The little dog had been brave and had earned his freedom. Grinning, toothlessly, the old squaw held the dog over the meat pot. Holdin' to one hind leg she clubbed the animal over the head and dropped it in, hair and all! I couldn't stand it! I covered my mouth with both hands and turned away. Pizi was watching me scornfully.

"White-eyes dog sick, mebbe? By um by, injun kill em white-eyes dog! Take long time kill'em slow! Wagh!" He spat contemptuously, toward me. I took my hand away from my mouth. Suddenly, I felt the old burning, consuming flame in my brain. The next thing I knew, I was swinging my fists at the face of my enemy. I knocked him to the ground, but he leaped up quickly and whirled aside as I rushed in again, tripping me. He jerked out a knife and slashed at me. I rolled, barely avoiding the knife as it whistled past my throat. It was close, too dang close!

Making it to my feet, I faced the injun. Pizi held the knife low, slashing, bearing in as I back-pedaled.

"I kill White-Eyes dog!" screamed Pizi. "I kill now!" I was unarmed. My temper had gotten me into trouble and I had left my weapons in the lodge of Crazy Horse, hoping to show Red Cloud's people that I meant no harm to them.

I felt the burn of the blade as it grazed my forearm, then I grasped the knife arm of Pizi with both hands. I felt the old blackness blot out my mind as my self control was taken away from me. Pizi was shocked. This was a totally different white man than the brave had been fighting a moment before. My eyes blazed into the Indian's own black eyes. Pizi felt a feeling he had never felt before stir deep within him, fear!

Eyes glaring into his were the eyes of an animal, crazy with the lust for blood, and little red flecks danced and flared in their dark depths. A growl like the growl of a beast came from the throat of the white man. Slowly, the knife arm of Pizi was growning numb. Pizi realized with dismay that the blood supply to his hand was cut off by the terrible grip of the hated White-Eyes! A Gun roared, and cold snow sprayed over my combatants legs.

"You would dare kill one who is my guest, Pizi?" Red Cloud thundered. "One who has come in peace and saves the life of your Chief? To kill one White-Eyes, would you blacken the honor of our people, the Lakota and the word of your Chief?"

"He is a White-Eyes dog!" hissed Pizi vehemently. "I kill!"

"If you must kill, kill our enemies not our friends!" Red Cloud's voice rang in the stillness. "Go from this man!" Crazy Horse stood beside the Chief, his rifle ready. I come to myself starin' at Red Cloud. He shore wasn't the same older man that I had picked up out of the snow back there in the mountains. This was a fierce old fighter, a warrior! Pizi glared at me out of hate-filled eyes and spat at my feet.

"Go!" Red Cloud commanded. Pizi turned and padded away toward his lodge. *Later, I will kill the White-Eyes dog.* He promised himself,. *'and the blood-letting will be very satisfying!'* Red Cloud placed his hand on my shoulder.

"Friend, you are a very brave man. There are few men who would brave the knife of Pizi! He has killed many enemies. Come, I will take council with my white friend of important matters. Perhaps you may find the answers Red Cloud seeks. Washte!"

I followed the Chief into his lodge. I waited until Red Cloud was sitting comfortable, then I sat down, crossing my legs like the Indians do. First, came the pipe and the kinnikinnick tobacco. We blew smoke to the four winds. There was always medicine to be made, the right ceremony to follow, lest the 'spirits' might get mad! All the injuns clothing and possessions were covered with 'medicine'paintings. This was for good hunting and protection in war. Animals that were fleet of foot and of great strength, such as the fox and the grizzly, were used for 'medicine' animals. Parts of the medicine animals were placed in a pouch and hung around the Indian's neck. This was supposed to give the wearer 'supernatural' powers. At last, Red Cloud put away the pipe and began to speak.

"Once, the buffalo was as the blades of grass upon the prairie. The land was rich and good. The waters were clear and beautiful, and full of fish. The Indian was happy, his belly full. The Lakota roamed an unspoiled land. The land belonged only to them. Now, the white man comes to steal our lands. He cuts the Indian's trees. He kills the buffalo, not to eat, but for the love of killing. Now the buffalo grow fewer each day. The Indian will soon starve! The beautiful waters are poisoned with the mud from the white man's digging for the yellow metal. The fish die! The white man has no respect for the land!"

"He only kills and destroys, and by doing so, he will soon destroy himself! I have tried to live at peace with the white man. But the white man does not want peace! He wants the Indian's land. They will fight for their lands. They will fight for their honor! The white man has no honor. He has no love for the land. He cannot speak the truth. His treaties are lies. The yellow metal he digs from the ground is his god! There is nothing he will not do to obtain it. What does my white friend reply to Red Cloud?"

I sat silent, asking myself what Pa would do in a situation like this. After a while, I got up and slowly spoke the words I think Pa would have said.

"My red brother speaks the truth. The white man does these things and more. He takes the injun's land. He takes what he wants because he is many, and the red man is few. His weapons are fierce and he has many, many guns. If a red man wants guns, he must get them from the white man. When the gun is broken he must go to the white man to get another. True the white man desires that which belongs to the red man. But is it not also true that the injun desires that which is the white man's? The red man desires guns, he desires steel for his arrowhead and most of all, he desires the white man's firewater! The red man trades his wives and his daughters for firewater. I ask you, is this honorable? The Great Spirit finds all his children fighting over that which he has created. The Lakota fought the Crow for his land and won. The Crow was defeated. He retreated to another part of the land, far from the Lakota.

The white man also fought for this land. He fought another strange nation that lives far across the great waters of salt. He defeated the French, he defeated the Spanish. The white man fought these peoples even while the Lakota fought the Crow. The French and the Spanish had to retreat back across the waters of salt. Now, only the white man and the red man are left to fight over the land.

The white man fights the red man and the white man will defeat the red man in the end, because he is strong and is as many as the leaves in the trees. I do not think the Great Spirit is pleased with his children. Perhaps he will turn his face away, and the world will die? I do not know. This I know, I wish to live at peace with those who would be my friends. I cannot speak for my people. I can only speak as Red Cloud's friend!" I fell silent, waiting.

Red Cloud's head was bowed.

"White-Eyes speaks with great truth. You speak with wisdom and you speak with honor. But for those who would make war upon you, you will fight, for you are a man. What man is he that will not fight for his children, his land or his honor? The Crow has retreated to another place, but the Lakota has no place to go. The white man desires not part, but all that the Indian has, even his life. Would you surrender your children, your home, and your honor, simply because your enemy is stronger? I think not! The Lakota has no place to go. We will fight and we will die. But if we must die, let us ride the honor trail and die with honor. Hokahey, it will be a good day to die!"

I stared at the old Chief. He was a man and would fight and would die. No man could do more for his home and his woman. Suddenly, I was mad clear through. My home, and my woman, was back in Texas. I'd go back and fight even if I got hung for it! I noticed the similarities of Pa and Red Cloud.

'Son, do what is honorable and right, and ye'll never be ashamed to look any man in the eye!"

"Hokahey," I said to Red Cloud. "It will be a good day to die!"

"If all white man were like you, my friend, I think we could live in peace! Ho Ha He, my son!" The old Chief turned away, staring into the lodge fire. I don't think he knew when I left him. Walking slowly back to Crazy Horse's lodge, upon entering, I was careful to go directly to my place by the fire. Thus I figured I was starting to think like and Indian, learning the ceremonies, the customs, and the magic signs. When I first came here I had been very foolish, a greenhorn at injun ways. A day or two after I had been brought to the village, me and Crazy Horse had been visiting Red Cloud in his lodge. Foolishly, I had started to walk between the old Chief and the fire. At the time, I was admiring a beautiful beaded belt that was hanging from the lodge pole and I wanted a closer look. As I rose from where I was sitting, Crazy Horse pulled me back down, shaking his head. I was puzzled, but somehow I was smart enough to stay put. After the visit was over, and we were outside the lodge, I popped the question.

"O.k. what did I do? Did I move at the wrong time or something?" Crazy Horse sighed and tried to explain to me. It turned out that everyone occupying a lodge had their place to sleep, sit or eat. The place at the back of the lodge belonged to the host, or part of the hosehold. It was considered a grave insult to pass between the fire and this place of authority while it was occupied by the owner. Crazy Horse had saved me from committing this breach of conduct.

"This is Indian way, Indian custom. This mean you have respect for owner of lodge. If you crossed between Grandfather and fire, he would be greatly insulted. Somctimes this cause big fight, offends honor!"

"Seems like a lot to do over nothin'." I commented.

"You also have customs that are strange to the Indian, White-Eyes! Indian like to gamble, what if he play bones while in your house of God? Would it not be a great insult?

What if Indian want to eat and it not mealtime? Indian eats when he is hungry, white man only at meal time. Is this not a lot of to do over simple act of eating?" Crazy Horse gestured eloquently. I grinned. I was beat again! Even though I agreed with most of the Indian's grievances with the white man, my sympathies with the squaws lot, sometimes caused me trouble. Nearly all the hard labor around the village was 'squaws work'. The squaws wasn't no more than slaves to the man. The men did nothing but hunt, fight and gamble. They were real fond o' the bone game.

There was one particular time that I got in trouble over a squaw and it seemed like it was always this one particular squaw too. If'n ya get my drift. It went this way.

Crazy Horse and some of his buddies were fixin' to go on a little raid against the Crow. Now, like I said before. Injuns can't do nothin' without makin' a lot of fool medicine before hand. Since I was invited to this particular little shindig I didn't have any choice but to go through the same foolishness that Crazy Horse and his boys did. Seems like one of the tribe medicine men got it into his head that this raid was doomed to fail unless everybody took a sweat bath.

Well, the sweat lodge was built and prepared. A large fire was built outside the lodge. Several stones were heated to red hot and carried inside, being placed in a hol dug in the center of the floor. Cold water was then poured over those stones to make the lodge fill with steam. Right about then, is where we come in, naked! There just wasn't any other way to take a steam bath and bein naked was it! The medicine man said so. Nobody could wear even a breech clout or the big medicine would be ruined for sure. I didn't like it, but that's the way it was. Crazy Horse always held out a little information from me, seems like.

We set there a' lookin' straight ahead with our arms folded. Nobody was allowed to talk, laugh or even snicker. Medicine was some serious business with the Lakota. The steam was supposed to cleanse our bodies and make us holy, or somethin' like that We were settin in a circle around the hot stones and the steam was so thick I couldn't breath. I was sweatin' and my eyes were burning' out. On top of it, I was dying to sneeze, but I wasn't allowed to, which gives you some idea of the fun I was havin' playin' injun. Just when I thought I couldn't stand it anymore, Crazy Horse pointed to the door. Then bucks cut out a' there runnin' like a herd of buffalo straight for the river. Now, that was another little thing that Tashunka Witko had failed to tell me. Somebody had broken the ice and the dark grey water rippled under a cloudy winter sky. We ran barefoot over the frozen snow and when we got to the river Crazy Horse. yelled, "Hieeee!" and dove in.

Then I was sailin' through the air and hittin' that cold water and when my body reacted to it, it was like hitting solid ice! Anything that cold couldn't have been water! I felt like I was passin' out, but then I hit the surface gaspin' and swimmin' hard. The first thing I see was that dang redskin that had gotten me into this little deal in the first place. I took out toward Crazy Horse thinking about maybe pulling him under and drowning him. I dove, trying to sneak up under him from below. I grabbed at brown legs but all of a sudden he just wasn't there. I found out where he was when his arm grabbed me around the neck and pulled me under. The rest of the braves joined in and we had a fine time splashin' and rasslin'. Breaking the surface I saw the grinning face of Red Cloud's nephew.

"White man swim slow like turtle, or mebbe rock!" The

other braves roared. I had to laugh too, I guess. Then I noticed that we weren't the only ones laughin'! There was a bunch of injun girls standin' on the bank laughin' too! They giggled and put their hands over their mouths, and made motions as if they were drowning.

For some reason I thought that maybe they were laughing at me. I was beginning to get embarrassed when I saw her. *'Why, she's beautiful!'* I stared at a young injun girl that stood apart from the rest. She had a pair of hide buckets of water in her hands. Straight and slender, she stared back with a half smile on her face. *'She doesn't laugh like the others.'* I wondered. I was so taken by the girl that my open mouth filled with water and I started choking and strangling. Crazy Horse hooted and pointed at me.

"White-Eyes much stare at pretty squaw, he forget to swim! Haieeee! Me call White-Eyes coughing turtle!" The braves were having trouble swimming themselves that were laughing so hard. Then all the laughing stopped. Pizi was standing on the river bank, scowling.

"You go!" he growled, cuffing the girl with the buckets. She hurried away among the lodges, looking back real scared of Pizi. He stood and glared toward me for a minute, then he took after the girl, threatening and grunting. I didn't like it, I didn't like it at all! I looked at Crazy Horse. He knew what I was thinking.

"Her slave, belong to Pizi! White friend like pretty girl, hey? "

"What's her name?"

"Yo'wesa! It mean little cat." Crazy Horse grunted, "Hopo, let's go, water too cold. Go sit by fire, play bone game." I couldn't stand it. I sat by the fire thinking about the girl and Pizi. He was probably beating her right now. Crazy Horse looked at me two or three times with them black eyes of his, then he shook his head.

"Heap trouble come, me betcha!" He was right, as usual, seems like everytime I went anywhere around camp, I was bumping into that girl. Once, I met her on the trail outside of the village. She was carrying firewood for Pizi's fire. When I took her burden and was carrying it for her, she ran alongside me crying,

"No, no! He will beat me, I must carry it. Give it to me! Go away!" But I couldn't go away and someone told Pizi about it. He beat her again. This angered me so much, Crazy Horse and two of his friends, Man Afraid of His Horse, and Thump, a Hunkpapa had to hold me down. Still, I almost got loose, except for spotted Elk.

"Ehhh! He is strong, like Grizzly!" Hump growled. "It is the law, White-Eyes. If you interfere, both you and the girl will be killed. It is the law!

"Is this true?" I asked Crazy Horse.

"It is true, my friend. It is tribal law. No one can carry a slave's burden or give her assistance except her captor. She belongs to him. She is his slave."

"What can I do?" I pleaded and Crazy Horse replied

"You want girl?" I looked at him.

"Yes!"

"I fix!" beamed Crazy Horse. He quickly strode away, but was back in a minute, grinning broadly. "Is done!" he said simply.

"He's going to give her up?" I couldn't believe it.

"No! Long time Pizi, look at your horse. Him want bad. Make heap good warhorse. Big stallion, much strong." I was shocked to my toes.

"You.....Y'.. You mean, you traded my horse... You gave him Pa's stallion? No! I'll fight him first!

"No worry, White-Eyes, no trade appaloosa. Make bet

with Pizi. Big horse race tomorrow! You win race, you get girl."

"But what if I lose?" I had to ask even though I dreaded the answer.

"Him get stallion!" Crazy horse didn't blink an eye. I groaned. Crazy Horse slapped me on the back. "No worry, big horse win race. Pizi's pony way too slow. Appaloosa win. Aieeee! Him great spotted horse!" Crazy Horse took off.

"Goin' ta spread the news, I guess. Well, that danged red skin has done it again. I'm up to my elbows in trouble, cause o' him bettin' my hoss!" *'Course, I guess I was a little to blame. I couldn't blame it all on Crazy Horse.* I thought of Yo'wesa, and then I thought of my Diablo. It dawned on me, if I lost the race, Pizi would own them both! I must not lose, I gritted fiercely through clenched teeth!

The next day the whole tribe was out to see the show. It wasn't hard to see that my *'devil horse'* was the favorite to win. The way some of these bucks bragged on him, you'd have thought that Diablo was their horse!

"We race to big rock on hill!" Pizi grunted and pointed. Now, I guess I that I am not too trustin' with folks, as Pa told me not to be. You gotta always ask yourself if what they're doin' is on the up an' up! The pinto that Piza was goin' to ride was standin' there hipshot an' sleepy lookin'. I had taken another look at that pony an' I noticed the strong shoulders, the small, solid hoofs, and cannon bones. It was a wild caught mustang an' I knew somewhat about mustangs. Seein' as how me and Pa had tried catchin' an' breakin' em several times. They were tough an' sure-footed as a mountain goat over rough ground. They could do pretty well on the getaway, too.

After givin' the pinto the once-over, I took a good look

at the race course. It looked to be about a quarter mile
there an' back, with rocks and boulders scattered all along
it. The going was steep and rough as a cats tongue. My big
stallion would shore be at a bad disadvantage, but how was
I to get out of it? I didn't know. Thinkin' about it for a
minute, I had me an idea, alright! I put my hands on my
hips, laughing and shakin' my head.

"No! That's too short, and too easy! Let's make it a real
race. Let's go to the far cottonwood across the stream over
there and then back to here. The first one to pass the lance
wins!" Now that cottonwood was a good half mile at the
least, down the valley, an another half mile back. That
added up to one long flat mile, which would be just what
the Appaloosa could handle the best. I waited. Crazy Horse
grunted and looked at Pizi.

"No! Is too far! No good!" Pizi wasn't a dummy when it
came to horses, either! I knew just what to say to clench the
deal. I smiled an' I said,

"What's the matter, Pizi, are you afraid that your horse
cannot win? Is your pony wind broke? Such a short
distance as you ask is for colts that still suckle at their
mothers teets! Great horses deserve a great race! Do you
not agree, my friend?"

"I am not your friend." Pizi said vehemently. I had him
over a barrel and he couldn't do anything about it. Pizi had
to accept or lose face before the whole tribe.

"Hopo!" he said, "let's go!" Crazy Horse plunged his
lance deeply into the ground.

"Washte, good! This finish line! Get ready brothers!"
Low Dog, a tall, skinny injun, held up his hand and
shouted.

"Get ready!Aiiieee!" He brought down his arm hard!
"Hoka hey!" The shout from the people echoed across the

valley and Diablo leaped forward powerfully. The stallion was strong, but that sleepy lookin' pinto charged into a bolt o' lightnin'! He darted away like a sparrow the second Low Dog's arm fell.

"That little horse can run!" I breathed. "But not like you can boy! He's the sparrow, but you're the hawk! I bent low and yelled in the stallion's ear. "Go boy! Go you devil horse!" Diablo flattened his ears and with an angry demeanor in his eyes, he targeted that pinto in front of him. I felt his breaths grow deeper within his big chest, enough that it felt he could bust. The resulting power from my horse took my breath away. He cut into the wind with lengthening, quickening, powerful strides that came faster and faster. There was still some snow patches here and there along the meadow. Diablo drank the cold air as he flew along and I could feel the cold wind whipping my face.

The pinto's pumping hind quarters in front of us was getting closer and closer! We reached the stream and it was up and over! My blood began to tingle. I started to laugh and shout like a crazy man!
I'd heard Pa tell about a race of men that lived way back in the past. He said they were called Vikings or men from the north. They loved to fight just for the thrill of it. He told me these fellers would just laugh an' sing whilst they were in the joy of battle! This must have been how they felt! I was enjoying this so much.

As we started around the cottonwood, it was neck and neck. Diablo had caught up to the Pinto. Foam from the pinto's efforts splattered my face. Standing up in the stirrups, I yelled out of pure adrenaline! The stallion heard me and flattened his ears even more. The great heart of that Appaloosa pumped the blood of the Nez Perce' war horses. It grew hot with the lust for battle! He ran as his ancestors had run the buffalo! The wind from the speed we were traveling caused the water in my eyes to start trailing out the corners. As Diablo lowered his shoulder and began reaching out even further with his neck it felt as if I were on top of a locomotive with only a piece of twine to stop him with. I began to worry if he tripped I would be dun for! Each stride I could feel his power propelling us faster!

The big stallion's mouth was now opened savagely, with the blood lust upon him .His nostrils flairing red, drawing in huge gulps of air and his lungs filled. Lungs which no mustang can have! Air makes speed! He screamed a challenge to the pinto as he swept away relentlessly and passed the lance three full horse lengths ahead of Pizi and his pinto. Diablo had gone plumb crazy wild! I had to rein him down, hard, to keep him away from the Indian ponies! Screaming and rearing, he pawed the earth with his hooves wanting to fight, his body trembling, his eyes rolling and his nostrils all red and flaring I wondered at my horse's power as he moved beneath me. Finally, I looked around and the people were going wild.

"Aieeeee! Hoka hey!" The tribe roared their approval! They paid my horse the tribute of the Sioux cry for great courage!

"H'gun, H'gun!' they chanted as Red Cloud raised his arms to the sky and shouted,

"Truly today, the Lakota have seen a great horse! The Great Spirit Wakan Tanka would be pleased to own such a horse! A great spotted medicine horse!"

"Aieeeee! H'gun, H'gun!" the people cheered. Pizi glared at me and his hate was like a living breathing thing! He drew his knife, and he leaped forward, to the mustang. The pinto stood on splayed legs with his head down and was covered in foam. With a cry of rage, Pizi cut the throat of that pinto! He turned, and he screamed again, out of pure hate and meanness! He then charged away toward his lodge.

Pizi's action sickened me. I stood ashen thinkin' that his actions shown that he shore was a poor loser. I felt so sorry for the little mustang! It had ran its heart out for him just like my horse did for me. Again, this was how mercy was not a normal part of the Indian's constitution.

The rest of the day was filled with slaps on my back for the win by the tribes' people. So much so it became sore. Many offers for the stallion were given. I would graciously decline them tho.

"He is my brother and one does not trade his brother." I would tell them. The braves understood. Everybody invited me to their lodge for supper, and I turned em' down because I was still remembering that dog!

After I rubbed down the stallion with dried grass, I followed Crazy Horse to the lodge. When we got there he wouldn't go inside. He turned to me and declared,

"The lodge is yours! I have no squaw and a man with a squaw should have a lodge." Grinning broadly.

"She is not my squaw!" I protested.

"Truly, she is your squaw! For I have seen her look at you the way the braves of the Lakota look at your horse!" The young Indian smiled.

"Be brave my friend! May the Great Spirit protect you!" Then he was gone, to sleep in his uncle's lodge! I entered the tepee reluctantly. Here was another one o' them fool fixes I'd gotten myself into. *'Course it was the only way I knew of getting Yo'wesa away from Pizi before he killed her'*. I didn't have any doubts about it, either. Pizi was too full of hate to ever treat anything or anybody right. He'd destroy everything around him just like the pinto! The little horse had done the best he could, but Pizi cared for nothing but winning and feeding his hatred.

Yo'wesa rose from the willow mat and came toward me. She looked at me shyly, and then kneeled at my feet.

"You have taken me from Pizi and my heart is glad, for you are a good man. I will serve you well." She kept her eyes downcast, as a proper slave should. I didn't like it. I didn't like for grovelin' at my feet like I was her master. It gave me a bad feelin'

"Git up from there! Yore free! You ain't nobody's slave no more, dang it"! My irritation had made me speak more harshly than I meant to. Yo'wesa gasped, and fled from the lodge. That night she came slippin' into the lodge like a fugitive.

"I am sorry, for I have angered you. Yo'wesa work hard, cook, carry wood! You see!" I had messed up my first try at makin' her understand, so I took her by the shoulders gentle-like, an' tipped her head up so I could look down into her face. She was a slim little thing, like a deer, all shy an' bashful.

"Yo'wesa, you are free. I do not wish you to be my slave. I only want you to be happy. If anybody, carries wood around here, it's gonna be me. That kind of work is too hard for a little thing like you. And another thing, if any cookin's done around this lodge, it better not be dog!" She looked at me.

"You are strange man. You not like dog?"

"No! You must not do that Yo'wesa." She didn't wait to hear no more, she just smiled at me real teasin' like.

"You no like it, white man?" She looked at me, and I didn't like the look in her eye. I knew then that it was my turn to be hittin' for the door! Quick as I got out, I looked around as mean as I could. There'd better not be no body eave's droppin', like one Crazy Horse and his friends! I didn't see anyone, so I went around the back way. Feelin' a bit cowardly and sneaky, I had to do somethin'.

The situation was gittin' embarrassin' and it was shot full o' trouble for one Rainey. If the Lakota found out, they might misunderstand, and they think I was spurnin' Yo'wesa 'cause she was an injun! I'd seen how these child-like children of the wild could change suddenly into savage, cruel and merciless killers at the drop of a hat. I'd seen 'em torture Crows an' other captives at the stake, burnin' and punchin' out their victims eyes with fire brands! They'd skin prisoners alive, an' a lot of the other things too mean to mention. It'd go hard for me if they misunderstood. I walked around for a while trying to think of a way out of my problem, but aside from hittin' the trail, I couldn't find none.

Finally, I headed back to the lodge. I'd just have to make Yo'wesa understand. She was sittin' on a blanket by the fire when I entered. She did not raise her head. I waited for her to speak, but when she didn't I realized that I would have to.

"Why do you not speak, Yo'wesa?"

"I am shamed before my people," she moarned. "You turn me away. I have nowhere to go."

"No! You shall not be shamed before the people. I have not turned you away. You shall stay here in this lodge with me!"

"But why, if you do not want me for your woman, why did you take me from Pizi?"

"Because I want you for my sister, Yo'wesa, one as pretty as you shall be my sister, not my woman. Far away to the south I have a woman. She is here, always in my heart."

I held my hand over my chest and then walked out.

Yo'wesa watched her young White-Eyes leave and whispered to herself,

"It is not enough!" she sighed. "I do not feel like a sister! Your woman is far away, white man, and I am here!" Yo'wesa smiled then and stretched like a little cat. "Yes! She is far away, and I am here!"

13

~ <u>RED JOHN'S DILEMMA</u> ~

*J*ori Lee sat on the big, moss covered, boulder, dangling her feet in the cool current. The water made little musical, liquid sounds as it tumbled, splashing over the colored stones.

"Singing its way to the sea," Jori whispered. She saw the big trout rise from his home under the boulder. He sucked in a foolish grasshopper that was flying too close to the water.

Remembering, she could almost hear the squeals of laughter and joy on hot summer days gone by. She and Rance had played pirates and the boulder had become swift pirate's sloop of war. They had flown the Jolly Roger from the top of the old pine, and many a treasure had been secreted away in the cave under the waterfall. Enemies had been slain by the thousands, and the old trout was a whale that surfaced alongside their ship.

"There she blows!" Rance would cry out when the trout rose to feed. Jori remembered the day he had caught the trout. It was a trophy to thrill any boy's heart. But Jori Lee had looked up at him, tears welling up in her eyes, and begged him to turn the trout loose.

"Please Rance, for me? Please?" Rance had hung his head guiltily under her pleading eyes and he mumbled,

"Guess our place wouldn't be the same without this ol' trout livin' under that big rock. Shore, Jori, I'll put the ol' booger back for you." Jori loved him with her eyes while she watched the trout dart swiftly back to his home. Smiling secretly to herself, she remembered how she had teased the bashful boy until he had hung his head in misery

"Shore, my knees is long and I guess I'm ugly, too. Too ugly to be swimmin' with a purdy gal like you, Jori Lee." Feeling sorry, she'd put her arms around his neck.

"Oh Rance, it was all in fun. You are not ugly, and don't you dare say that you are! Why you're about the handsomest boy as any girl could ever want!" Then she had kissed him fiercely on the lips. It was wild and sweet, and that ache that throbbed deep within her heart grew bigger and bigger until it threatened to consume her, body, soul, and spirit.

Breathless, she'd torn herself away, seeing not the bashful, moody boy of before, but a man! A man, whose eyes burned with desire and love. Springing forward, Rance had sought to take her into his arms again. Laughing, Jori Lee dove into the pool, leaving him standing there on the rock, staring with those intense dark eyes.

Her memory began to be painful. Jori Lee Rainey looked around at the pool with tears glistening in her eyes. The cottonwoods rustling in the wind was whispering a song in cadence with the beat of her heart.

"Alone…. I'm alone…He's gone! Oh Rance, will I ever see you again?" Her voice broke, and she buried her face in the cool moss and cried.

Up at the house, Libby was washing dishes.

"Jori Lee's not much help anymore, poor lil' thing. She's missin' the boy, an' I guess I know how that feels. I miss Bill, too. Love is a mighty hard thing on a person. I guess me an' Jori is about the loneliest two people in Texas! Oh well, Elizabeth," she said to herself, "Hurry up and get the job done!"

Finishing up, she wiped her hands on the pink and white apron around her waist. She took it off and opened the front door to the late evening sunshine. Leaving it open, she swept the porch, and then she leaned the broom against the log door jam. She walked absent mindedly over a little well-trodden path to a grove of cottonwoods. Under the cottonwoods, a weathered grave marker stuck up slantingly. She knelt by the grave. The inscription read

"William Rainey,"
"Beloved Father and Husband"
"1835-1871"

"He was a good man." Libby whispered. "Oh Bill, What am I goin' to do? I need you so. Rustlers have cleaned us out, and Mr. Swain down at the bank wants his money. Every hand we hire is scared off the place, or is shot down from behind. The sheriff won't do 'nothin, an' I'm at my wit's end. Jori Lee is pinin' herself away over the boy, and if he doesn't return soon I don't know what she'll do. She loves him, Bill, like we loved each other." She touched the weathered marker gently.

Black-eyed susan's nodded their blooms sleepily on their stems and green grasshoppers buzzed in the spring sun.

Hearing the gallop of a horse, she rose from where she was sitting beside her husband's grave and walked hurridly back to the house. Her eyes narrowed as she shaded them from the sun.

"It's that no account sheriff, come to order us off the place!" She retrieved the broom from the door jam and stood on the top of the steps watching the sheriff rein in his horse, getting stiffly down from the saddle.

"Save yourself the trouble, Dexter, an' git back on yore ol' nag and dust out o' here! I know what you're here for so they ain't no use in your sayin' it, so go on an' git!

"Now, Miss Rainey, I'm the law round h'yar an' what I say goes! Ya know I got ta do muh job. I's jest doin' muh job. They ain't got no call fer you to bring some trouble down on ya than ya already got, nowdays. Ya know the mortgage on this place is up at midnight tomorrow night an' Mr. Swain down at the bank had ta have th' money or else foreclose on yore spread. Ya'll be better off anyways. This h'aint no fit place for two women alone. Ya got your daughter ta think of. H'it don't look right you an' her livin' way out h'yer with a greaser, ya know. Why, it aint proper like!" Libby eyed the sheriff distastefully.

Juan is our hired man and he's almost seventy years old now, Dexter, and it danged well aint anyone else's business!" Dexter was all that Elizabeth Jane would condescend to call the sniveling runty sheriff. He hadn't been elected by vote, anyway. After the War Between the States, Dexter had kow-towed and licked the boots of the carpet baggers and crooked politicians. He had gotten himself appointed sheriff, and it wasn't too hard after that to get his half brother, Periwinkle, appointed district schoolmaster. *But there wasn't anything law abiding about the two,'* thought Libby angrily. Especially Dexter!

All the ranches were losing cattle, and Dexter had yet to catch a single rustler! He wasn't man enough to be called Mister and darned if she was going to call him sheriff!

Libby advanced on the fat, sweating man, noticing his uncleanliness. Malodorous to the extreme, baggy, sweat-stained breeches topped his down at the heel boots. Tobacco rivulets stained his beard above an open, grimy shirt. Red, sweat-stiff, long-johns were visible to the waist. She raised the broom threateningly.

"Now Dexter, you git an' git!, Pronto! You ain't even got manners enough to take your hat off when you're talkin' to a lady!" Libby Jane whacked the sheriff across his battered hat. Her broom fairly whistled, and she hit him again as he ran splay-legged for his horse. He ran with his arms thrown up over his head and shoulders, trying in vain to ward off the blows.

"Ow! Dad blame it, woman! No, cut it out! Ouch!"

"This here ranch is mine until midnight tomorrow night, so I'm orderin' the likes o' you off and pronto! Git, Dexter!" Elizabeth Jane Rainey was mad, and she was truly a picture of robust, firey womanhood as she laid into the sheriff.

"Woah, hoss," Red John McDonald pulled up his animal under the cottonwoods. He grinned. "That shore is a' lot a' woman! I reckon I'll jest set h'yer an' watch the fireworks, heh, heh! Be still, hoss, 'afore I fall off, dad burn it!" From where John sat his horse, the distance was about thirty yards, to the *fireworks*, as he put it. If he had looked down and over to the side, he'd have seen the wooden grave marker on Bill Rainey's grave. He leaned over against the big cottonwood lazily and began to pack his pipe as he watched and chuckled to himself.

The sheriff had finally managed to mount the crowbait

that he called a horse and shook his fist at Libby Jane.

"Now see what you made me do, I done gone and swallowed my tobacky!" He choked and wheezed for breath. Then he scowled, reaching for his saddle gun, he began to draw the weapon. His little pig eyes glittered with murderous intent.

"Wouldn't be thinkin' of usin' that smoke-pole, now would ya', mister?" Red John's deep voice brought the sheriff up short. Dexter half-turned to look at the business end of Red John's buffalo gun.

"This ol' guns killed a' heap of buffler an injuns! She makes a gosh awful hole, and she's got a' har' trigger, too! Used to be set a little better, but she's wore now and it don't take much to set 'er off!" The sheriff's mouth went dry and he blanched. He'd seen men shot with them ol' needle guns. It could well nigh turn your stomach, and not from swallowing tobacky, either. He let the rifle slide back into its saddle scabbard, and spread his hands placatingly.

"N-N-Now, take it easy, mister, I wasn't meanin' the lady no harm, honest! I's jest checkin' muh riggin', thet's all!"

"Bye mister!" Red John rumbled ominously. The sheriff turned pasty white.

"Wh- what yuh mean to do? Ye can't ...er, yore not gonna..."

"Dust yore breeches an' ride!" Red John McDonald thumbed. The sheriff whirled his horse and took out a' spurrin' an a' slapping' the poor animal on the flanks with the end of his reins. He rode like he'd never rode before. He didn't know who that red-headed feller was, but the look in his eye was easy to understand. Sheriff Dexter counted himself lucky to be alive.

After putting a safe distance between himself and the

ranch house, he pulled up in the shade of a boulder. He wiped his brow with a grimy sleeve.

"Mebbe he's a' mean hand the lady's hired. If'n he is, I'm gonna take pertick'ler pleasure in havin' him gunned down." He grinned, showing jagged, rotten teeth. "Buck'll fix him fer his medlin', hee, hee! Yep! Ol' Buck's fixed a' lot of 'em. I ain't never seen him miss, not never!'"

It was still a long way to town. Sheriff Dexter squinted at the sun. It was still early. He had time for a quick snooze. Getting down from the horse, he stretched out in the shade. Leaving his horse standing in the sun, the sheriff was soon snoring heavily. The horse swished his tail at the flies.

The sun was hot, but the animal had been a cowpony and was well trained. It stood miserably, tied just as surely to the spot by the ground hitch as if to a hitching post. Kindness was not one of the sheriff's virtues. Come to think of it, the sheriff had only one driving impulse. Greed! The horse swished again at flies and the sheriff went on snoring in the shade.

Jori Lee saw the sheriff when he rode by like a mad man. She stared, and then ran for the house, holding up her skirts.

"Ma, what's wrong? I just saw the sheriff tearin' down the road like th' devil was after him." Jori Lee stopped up short, breathless when she saw the strange man with her ma.

"Ain't nothin wrong, honey." Libby soothed, "Nothing a'tall." Jori looked at Red John suspiciously.

"Who's he?"

"The devil!" Libby looked at Red John and grinned. Jori looked at them both with her mouth open, then she saw that both were about to burst out laughing. She stamped her foot.

"Awww, Ma, yore funnin' me!" Elizabeth Jane smiled at Red John.

"Light an' set stranger. Supper's on in a minute. Ya' kin wash up out back of the house."

"Thank ye kindly, ma'am." John dismounted and dusted his hat. "I come a' long way an' a hot meal is plumb welcome!" Jori stood dumbfounded! Her ma shore wasn't one to go around invitin' strange men into the house.

"Ma, will you puleeze tell me what's goin' on 'round here?"

"Later child, later," said Libby, while rushing around the kitchen, banging pots, and pans. She stopped a moment and smiled, and then started right back into rushing around again. Jori watched her ma with misgivings. Libby was acting like she had eaten loco weed!

'What in the world has gotten into Ma?' she thought. *'It's too early for supper! We always eat right on the dot at six!'* The young girl cocked her head sideways and grinned to herself. *'That red- headed man! Ma's gone, big-eyed over him! Well, I never thought I'd see the day...'*

Red John washed up in the chipped, enamel wash basin provided on a split log bench in back of the house. The pitcher was full of water and there was a nice clean towel, too. After drying his hands, John noticed that the 'towel' looked suspiciously like a piece of a woman's nightgown, or undergarment. He hung the towel up to dry and watched old Juan lead his horse away after taking off the saddle.

Turning back to the bench, Red stared into the piece of cracked mirror that lay on it's rough surface. He rubbed his beard thoughtfully. *'Mebbe I ought ta' shave. It shore wasn't every day a man's got 'vited to set down to vittles in a real honest-to gosh kitchen. An' them two women were shore 'nuff lookers.'* John thought about the fiery one with the pretty golden hair. She had spunk, and the way she'd stood up to that lawman, pleasured the mountain man. *'Fancy and sweet,'* John smiled. *'Mighty handsome, mighty handsome,'* He thought to himself, enraptured. *'Yeah, h'its only proper ah'm shore I ought to shave!'* And he did, for the first time in seven years!

Libby studied the big man who ate so heartily. He had red, curly hair, broad shoulders, and blue eyes. He looked to be in his late thirties, but he wasn't old, not too old at all! He was probably scot-irish, with all that red hair. She liked the way he smiled, real slow and friendly. Yes, Elizabeth Jane Rainey decided that she defiantly liked the man.

"What did you say your name was, mister, uh…"

"McDonald, ma'am. Red John McDonald, an' ah'm beholdin' to ya for the fine fixin's. It's been quite a' while since ah had vittles like these here. Ah'm afraid thet I've kinda over done mahself. Ah'm beggin' yore pardon, ma'am!"

"Oh not at all Mr. McDonald, not at all! I like a man that eats hearty. Will you have another piece of pie? There's plenty more!" Libby Jane smiled sweetly. Red smiled back forgetting the pie. All his attention was on his beautiful hostess.

"Well," Jori Lee said to John. "Aren't ya gonna take the pie, mister?"

"Oh!" John got hold of himself. "Yeah! Shore! If'n you insist, ma'am."

"John," Libby said. "My name is Elizabeth. Elizabeth Jane Rainey, you may call me Libby," she said kindly. Jori Lee was flabbergasted. *The both of them were grinnin' just like two possums in a 'simmon tree. An' that Red John! Why, he'd eaten a' whole pie by himself!'* Jori lee had never seen the like in all her born days. *'The way ma was actin', it was enough to turn your stomach, agggh!'* Jori asked to be excused so she could go down to the creek and sit.

"Right after you get through with the dishes, young lady. Libby said, getting up from the table. Red John got up, too, politely. "John and I will go sit in the living room beside the fire. Must'nt neglect our manners, er, I mean guests you know."Libby added, seeing Jori Lee's astonished face.

"Thank you kindly, ma'am." He smiled, as Libby took his arm and started to the living room. "Bye, Miss Jori Lee," he said, back over his shoulder.

'Now how did he know my name? I didn't hear Libby tell him? Oh well,' Jori Lee turned to the table and hurried to the task at hand. When she finished, she stepped out the back door and ran off to the comforting creek she had been longing to go to.

The sweet smell of pipe tobacco, rich and pungent filled the log ranch home. Red John puffed contentedly.

"In answer to your question ma'am, or, Libby, is yes, they's land to be had farther west. H'its mighty, fine land, rich and timbered in places. They's plenty of game an' water, But it's a wild land, tho, hard on men an' even harder on women. Ya got your girl to think about. I'm askin' ya' if'n you wouldn't be better off in town?"

"Mebbe you two could find employment, say clerkin' or start a real good eatin' place. Way you kin cook, ma'-er, Libby, you two would make out just fine. 'Sides, it's too dangerous fer a single wagon. They's injuns, flood, heat, an' bad men just fer starters. You'd never make it without a guide, neither! Ya gotta think about that, shore!

Oh, I'm thinkin' about it, John, I'm thinkin' about it real hard." Elizabeth Jane smiled sweetly. John choked, the legs of his chair banged down against the split log, pungeon floor. He looked at her, his eyes narrowed with suspicion. John didn't like the way she was lookin' at him. Rance hadn't told how to cope with a deal like this.

"Well, ah' gotta go an' check on my horse, ma-er, Libby! I reckon that I'll bed down in the barn meantime." John knocked out his pipe after rising from his chair. 'Eve'nin, Miss Libby, thanks kindly fer the pie. It shore was dee-licious! An' you a mighty handsome woman too!" Red John turned red all the way to the ears. *'Tarnation!'* Had he said that? *'Shore ya said that, ya ol goat!'* He thought as he hurriedly grabbed his hat from the peg on the wall.

"Why John, I think you for the compliment, and I think you're a fine figure of a man, too." John was having trouble swallowing by this time, and something was blocking his wind. He whirled, bumping into the door, then bolted out into the night. His face burned red. *Dratted fool! What had I gone and done that fer? Made a danged fool of myself, thet's what I'd done! What'd Rance think if'n he knowed his friend was makin' up to his ma?'* John walked along the stream reluctant to bed down, pondering how to tell them about the kid. He stood underneath a large, old pine, studying the stars. He listened to all the night sounds, crickets singing, the water rushing, and there was a funny sound, all soft and muffled. It sounded much like a woman crying!

'Shore, an' I'll bet thet be Jori Lee, poor little thing! Reckon, I know who she's cryin fer. Well, h'its time to start doin' thet lookin' after the kid's folks like I'd promised. I know Rance jest asked me to check in on em' if'n I was ever in these parts. But I owe my life to the kid, and I'm gonna do my best! Shore you ol' fool,' John's conscience prodded at him. *'An' is that the only reason? Shut up!'* John argued with himself accidentally out loud. "Jest shut up!"

"Ohh!" Jori Lee Rainey lifted her head to see the huge

shape of the man against the lighter background of the night sky.

"'Scuse me, miss, ah wasn't meanin' to eavesdrop on you, but I reckon thet I got something' to tell ya thet ya might be a little interested in. If'n you will excuse me sittin down thar beside you, I'll git on with what I'm h'yer fer!" Jori Lee wiped her face and eyes with the back of her hand.

"What do ya mean, Mr.?"

"Red, gal, like ah said before, Red John McDonald. My father was a Scotsman, and my mother was Irish, an' purty she was, last I can remember. I ran away from home when I was ten. The old man was pretty hard on me an' strict so I lit out fer the west. Some folks said thet my granddaddy was a Scotts Clansman, and owned a castle or such. But I dunno, no matter. My name don't matter none. The name you'll be interested in is the name of a tall black haired young feller thet claims he's sweet on ya!"

"Rance!" Jori Lee's heart leaped in her breast! "Ohh! Mr. Red! Where is he. Is he alright? Nothin's happened to him? Ohh! Please hurry up an' tell me!"Jori Lee got upset rather easily.

"Kin ah set down, then miss?" John drawled.

"Oh, bother! Red John, if'n ya don't set down an' stop foolin' around, I'm gonna jest lose my temper!" Jori Lee stamped her foot. John set down real quick.

'Sorry Miss," he mumbled 'S'all right. Ever'thin's gonna be all right. Ol' Red John's gonna see to it, ye kin bet on thet!"

They left the next day at nightfall. Elizabeth Jane had no cattle left, and there was nothing John could do to help her keep the ranch. Libby gave old Juan the chickens and most of the furnishings of the house. He had bowed and smiled, his wrinkled old face seamed and puckered.

"Mucho gracious, senora. Juan thanks you again for your fine kindness." He plodded slowly away toward town, pulling the old hand cart that he had been pulling the day he had fist come to the ranch. The chickens clucked nervously in their wooden crates.

Libby lifted her eyes to the big man on the horse in front of the wagon. She smiled. Red John rode sullenly.

"Dratted woman, tryin to bring the whole she-bang, do dads an' all. He'd finally covinced them after beggin, cajoling and hollerin, to leave most of the stuff behind. Only by threatening to quit as guide had he won the argument. Still, John suspected that they had snuck some more things aboard while he wasn't looking. What could a man do, when a purty-yeller haired woman just smiled sweetly an' said, "Yes, John," then went on and done whatever she wanted to do in the first place?

"Jes' pays you no never mind," he grumbled. "Nursemaid to a milk cow, two she-males, an' a couple o' the stubbornest, hard-headedness mules ever spawned. How in Jehosphat did I ever git into these doin's, anyway?" Well, Com on," he yelled, grumpily, we aint got all day!"

"Yes John," Libby answered sweetly. She clucked to the mules. They flipped their ears and the old, but well-built wagon rolled a bit faster. The milk cow had to trot to keep up.

Back in town, Sheriff Dexter looked at his two cousins and rubbed his hands together.

"Now boys, h'yars whar we kill two birds with one stone, and git ourselves a nice little pay off, too. Hee, hee! I done got the gov'ner to raise that reward on that Rainey boy to three thousan' dollars! Now, all we got to do is foller thet widder and th' girl right to the boy. We stole the widder's cattle after ol' Oliver couldn't git his hands on th' ranch by marryin' her. She couldn't make the payments on th' mortgage without any cattle to sell. So, now old man Swain's got the place jest like he always wanted. Paid right handsome, too, he did! Now ya can't beat thet, now can ye? You two boys stick with me an' well do all night. Yes sir, hee, hee!"Buck Dexter set his whisky glass down on the table with a crash.

"Shut yore mouth, ya ol' fool!" He hissed. "You might be the law, but lawmen have been hung before. Jes' ask ol' Henry Plummer's widder how he swung in th' breeze! The word's out thet the cattlemen's association have hired 'em some Pinkerton's. I ain't ready to hang, yet, not by a long shot. If'n ya don't button yore lip, mebbe somebody will button it fer ya. These ol' ranchers round here would hang us high if'n they found us out!" He glared at the runty sheriff.

"Sorry," the sheriff mumbled. Jase and Buck Dexter were bounty hunters in between playin' deputy for the sheriff. Truth is, they were out and out thieves. The sheriff was recovered from Buck's rebuke and was feeling very smug with himself. Three thousand dollars was a lot of money. Jase and Buck was gonna help him get it. Dexter looked at the two. Buck was big, black-bearded with yellow eyes that bored straight through a man. Cruelty shone plainly on the man's face. He spoke to the sheriff again.

"How ya goin' ta' git away from town, you bein sheriff an all, cousin?"

'I'm leavin' ol' Barney in charge, he's pure dumb an' he don't know nothin about all this. He'll tell people thet I'm gone back to Missouri to see to my folk's buryin! Thet'll make th; fools sorry for me, an they'll hold my job fer me, hee, hee! Jase Dexter, the thin, sallow faced one with the watery eyes, spoke in his high-pitched voice.

"Well, what are we waitin fer? Let's go git 'em!" Jase fancied himself a bad man with a gun. He liked to kill and enjoyed the feeling of power and superiority watching one of his fellow human beings die in their own blood, especially if Jase had been the one to shed that blood. He wore his two guns tied down and low. Buck Dexter looked at his kid brother and scowled. Of the two, Buck was undoubtedly the most dangerous. He was big, and he was mean. A very bad man to fool with!

Sheriff Dexter knew them well. He'd ridden with them during the War Between the States. Renegades, castoffs and deserters from both sides, they prayed on the helpless, the weak, raping and taking what they wanted from the families of the men gone off to war. When the war ended, they had been smart enough to leave Missouri and come to Texas, leaving behind their dark identities, for new ones. They pretended to be veterans of the union army, displaying medals taken from the bodies they had plundered. Making sure to befriend the carpet baggers for the gains it would bring them. True, the people around about were southerners, but power was in the hands of the Yankee bankers and politicians.

Dexter and his two cousins were soon appointed to the local law, much to the people's chagrin. Buck Dexter growled,

"Let's go, cousin, we got us a little job to do!" They tromped from the saloon with the runty sheriff bringing up the rear. Dexter watched the back of Buck narrowly. *Yep, Buck and Jase was gonna git him that three thousand dollars. It was too bad they wasn't gonna live through it to get their share of the blood money!* The cattlemen were more than suspicious, an' the operation here was just about over. With what he had in the safe in the Marshall's office, Dexter could start over somewhere else out west. He'd just come back for the money, and then he'd resign and disappear. He wasn't fool enough to think things could go on here much longer. It was time to hang it up. He didn't like the way Buck treated him, anyway. *'No respect, No respect at all. Well, Buck was gonna die from Dexters bullet, in the back or whatever'*, the sheriff didn't care.

"Yeah," he mumbled to himself. "Hit's payday, boys, pay day fer ol' Dexter and death fer y'all, hee, hee!" The unsuspecting, Buck and Jase mounted and rode their horses' west leading pack horses, the sheriff still bringing up the rear. *'It's always been like that, me bringing up the rear. But that's all right. Sometimes h'it's the best thing now, ain't it?'* He chuckled, his little pig eyes, glittered with deadly amusement.

Buck Dexter felt the prickle's between his shoulder blades. He'd felt it before. Most times, right after him and Jase had quarreled, and he had turned his back on him. He knew he had wanted to kill him but Jase, so far, had held back. Deep down, Jase was a coward. That's why he liked to see things die. It gave him reassurance that he was strong and alive. Buck knew his kid brother. But it wasn't Jase that gave him that prickle down his back right now while Jase rode beside him. There was only one person behind Buck Dexter. The Sheriff!.

"I didn't think the old coot had it in 'em!" Buck mumbled.

"Huh, what did you say?" Jase querried absent mindedly.

"Nothin'!" Buck smiled a cold smile. His yellow eyes resembled a hunting cat's just before the kill. The sheriff was the prey. Even while he planned to kill Buck, he had become the pray instead of the hunter. Buck knew his intentions because of that sixth sense that a very few killers have. It was pure animal instinct. The sheriff was a dead man!

Well, in back of the three a fourth horse followed slowly, keeping to the trees and brush. In the saddle rode another man, a man with gray eyes, eyes which held the very same gleam as those of Buck Dexter. On his leather vest the big man wore a star. A U.S. Marshall's star!

14
~ AN INDIAN MARRIAGE ~

*M*y name is Crazy Horse, and I have heard the owl
cry out. There is sickness in the lodge of my white friend,
and his heart is heavy with sorrow. I know that the girl,
Yo'wesa, will not get well, as my friend insists. My friend is
a white-eyes and White-Eyes do not believe in Indian
medicine, but I have heard the owl cry out. Soon the spirit
of the princess will walk the path of the stars, and I am
sorry. She is my friend's woman.

The squaws say that she dies of a broken heart, because
her man will not lay with her. The old squaws are crazy. My
friend is a man! I know that he would not let such a
beautiful woman go to waste. They are foolish old women!
But, I speak foolishly, also. The girl is ill., and death has
come for her. All that has gone before does not matter. I sit
with my friend outside the lodge and I hear the rattles of
the medicine men. They have not heard the owl. I watch
the shadows inside the lodge skins move and dance in the
glow of the firelight. There is a scrape of talons in the trees
above as the owl flies silently to the lodge poles of my
white friend. The owl lights on them, shaking the poles

with his weight. It is a great horned owl. His yellow eyes blink in the firelight and the owl cries out again.

The shadows stop to listen and the rattles are silent. No longer does the wingbone whistles blow. The medicine men have heard the owl. The drums are still. Soon the medicine men will leave the lodge. They are afraid of death, afraid of seeing his face. Whoever sees the face of death will die. This is certain. The spirits have called, and the girl's spirit will obey. The owl lifts away from the lodge poles. I point, my friend has seen the owl also, but I can see in his eyes the disbelief. After all, he is only a white-eyes. They know nothing of the spirits. The medicine men hurry from the lodge quickly.

As I sit here outside the lodge that my friend Crazy Horse gave me and I watch their injun doctors leave. They were givin' up just 'cause an ol' owl had whoo-whoooed. It made me mad. 'Course, they might as well leave an' give th' girl some peace an' quiet. That would do her a lot more good than that caterwauling the medicine men had been doin'! Jest as soon as they were gone, ol' Watenay, Red Cloud's wife, come to the door of the lodge.

"Come, she is asking for you, my son." She stepped back as I enter the lodge. Crazy Horse remained outside the lodge politely, as it is the Indian custom. Yo'wesa still lay on the bed of robes where she had been laying for two days. I looked at Watenay. She shook her head, looking at me with pity in her eyes.

"She calls your name many times. It is the fever." Watenay turned then and left the lodge. I knelt down by the bed of robes.

"Yo'wesa! Little one, I am here." The girl's dark lashes fluttered open. She looked at me out of feverish eyes.

"Washte, it is good to see you my man!" The girl spoke

in a whisper. "You must forgive me. I have promised to serve you well, but now I lie ill on my skins." I took her hand in mine. It was very hot.

"Do not worry yourself with such things, an' there's nothin' to forgive! Just you need to be gettin' well soon." It broke my heart to see her this way. She was so small, so frail with the sickness. It was hard to believe she was Yo'wesa, the girl who could climb swiftly and run like the deer. Me an' her had hunted and fished together. We had followed the buffalo, and she had kept my lodge and made my clothes. She looked at me with love in her eyes.

"Do you love me?" she asked, with a weak smile.

"Yes, Yo'wesa, I love you, my sister."

"But I have not felt like your sister". She murmured. "I have loved you as my husband, even though we have not wed. Why do you not love me in this way?" she pleaded. I dropped my head. I felt guilty and low-down. I never had been able to make her understand. I have never wanted to hurt her. I was shook up by her heart-broken question.

"I love you because yore sweet and good, Yo'wesa! I do not wish to hurt you. Don't you understand?" I asked, feelin' terrible bad.

"I have heard the owl cry out." She stated simply. "Soon I must travel the path of stars. My spirit shall be one with them." I couldn't stand hearin' her talk like that.

"No!" I cried out.

"Shhhh!" Yo'wesa placed her fingers on my lips. "Do not cry out so, my man. I am not afraid to die. I but wish one thing before."

"What is it? I demanded, fool that I was.

"I'm gonna git it fer you if'n it kills me. My voice broke with anguish.

"You, my man, promise this? She asked.

"Yes!" I said, stroking her smooth cheek. "I promise." She looked at me for a long time.

"Please do not be angry with me, for I ask that you become my husband!" She dropped her eyes and I was struck dumb. I loved her but I loved Jori Lee, too. What could I do? I had given my word. Pa always told me to keep my word, no matter what. I was torn between my love for this girl and Jori Lee.

"It will only be for a little while." Yo'wesa added softly. "When I get to the path of stars, I will tell them of my wonderful husband, and my spirit will be happy. But I will not hold you to your promise if you do not wish it." Tears glistened in her dark eyes. "A spirit that dies in sadness remains unhappy forever!"

That did it! I had to do it. Whether I believed in the injun' religions or not, I couldn't let her die unhappy and with a broken heart. I said,

"Yes" so quiet that I didn't think she had heard me. Then she opened her eyes and gazed at me with a look so full of happiness I couldn't stand it. She smiled, and touched my face. The hand was feverish and hot.

I left the lodge to talk to Red Cloud. The ceremony must be quick no matter how long injuns medicine is supposed to take. Red Cloud objected to the idea.

"It cannot be, she is dying. You have only to wait a few hours more. Why do you do this?"

"I wish for her to be happy in the afterlife." Red Cloud stared at me with wonder.

"Can it be that you finally have learned to believe in our belief's, in our spirit world?

"Maybe," I grunted. The chief looked at me, and then sighed with resignation.

"So be it!" He went to the door of his lodge. "Summon

the medicine men. Tell them there is to be a marriage ceremony before dawn. Go swiftly!" The brave outside the lodge trotted away. Before morning Yo'wesa and I had become man and wife!

"Thank you, my husband,' she whispered when we was alone again. "My spirit will love you forever!"

"Do not talk of death." I said agonizingly. "Yore my wife now and ya gotta git well."

"I am sorry." she murmered weakly. She closed her eyes and was still for a while. It scared me.

"No! You do not deserve to die. You are a good and wonderful person. The spirits are wrong to take you!"Yo'wesa heard me.

"No, my husband, the spirits are always right." She looked at me strangely. "I would ask one thing more from you, my husband."

"What is it," I answered, glad that she was still alive. She dropped her eyes as if ashamed.

"I have heard of a custom between your people. It is something that a husband does with his wife when they are married."

"Yes," I mumbled feelin' mighty embarrassed. "It is called "Kissing. I would have you do so to me."she waited expectantly. I leaned over to her and kissed her softly.

"Again!" she demanded. This time the kiss was more like fire and she held me tightly to her. Her arms then weakened and she turned me loose. "Ohhh, it is a good custom!" She closed her eyes and sighed contentedly. Smiling and happy, she fell asleep. The owl called again, and death stalked to the tepee and entered. I ran away into the darkness and stayed away for a long time.

I was grieving, grieving for the spirit that walked the path of stars, happily telling them of her wonderful husband.

"There is not such a husband in all the world!" She'd be singing there as she danced across the Milky Way. I watched stars for a long time. A flaming star came shooting along its length. I was sure it was Yo'wesa. Suddenly, I felt peace, and I returned to the village. The lodge of death would be burned to the ground and for me, it was time to go home! I returned to the village andWatenay gave me food.

"You must eat, my son."

"Washte, Grandmother, you are a good woman. Red Cloud is lucky to have one such as you."She gave me a broad grin.

"Yes, I have told him so many times." Red Cloud entered the lodge and sat down in his place.

"We will smoke, my son." He motioned for his pipe. Watenay brought the beaded case, but inside I had placed a surprise. It had taken me right onto a month of hard work to carve it. Red Cloud brought out the present into the light.

"Haw, what is this?" It was a new pipe carved from red pipestone. The stem was wrapped in white and red beadwork. The mouth piece was of bone. Red Cloud handled the pipe reverently. "Wagh! It is great medicine!" He made a great show of packing the pipe of kinnikinnick, the injun's pipe tobacco. After smoking a while, the chief put his new pipe away.

"I have decided to give you an Indian name, do you accept?" I looked at him steadily. This meant that I would become one of the Lakota.

"Yes, Grandfather."

"Washte, Good! The medicine shall be prepared. But first," he looked at Watenay, who brought forth a bundle.

Inside were some of the fanciest injun duds I ever saw. There was a beautiful buckskin shirt that hung almost to my knees, beaded moccasins, and soft leggings. Everything in the bag was covered with precious beadwork and quills. All this was for me!

Yo'wesa, she make beadwork and tan skins, me help!" Watenay said brightly. Then seeing the pain in my face, she hurried to give me a striped saddle blanket. "This from Crazy Horse."

I had been hearin' somethin' scratchin' 'round outside the lodge an' I figured that I knew what it was. I bragged on the saddle blanket just as loud as I could.

"It is a fine blanket. It is too bad that Crazy Horse is not here, I wish to give him this many shoots in return." I held up the Spencer. Red cloud's eyes held amusement. He was onto the scratchin' too. There was a bump against the lodge skins and a grunt, then just about the time it takes for a young injun brave to hot foot it around the lodge, Crazy Horse came bustin' in. his eyes were glued to the Spencer. All of a sudden, he was a dignified injun. He walked over and stood stiffly in front of me. I placed the rifle in his hands along with the ammunition I had for the weapon.

"It is yours, my brother. It is not so fine as the saddle blanket, but will Crazy Horse accept?" The brave grunted that he would. I kind a' thought he might. A rifle like this un' was mighty hard fer an injun to git hold of. Crazy Horse would be a big man in the eyes of the other braves. He stalked to the entrance and went out. Me and Red Cloud eyed each other. It took just about enough time fore Crazy Horse to get outside an' take a deep breath, and produce the gosh-awfulest injun yell I ever heard! The sound of moccasins were pounding from ever' which way. Me an' Red Cloud went out to watch the show.

Crazy Horse was on his pony, ridin' up an' down the camp, firing the spencer an' yellin'. Purdy soon, they was a whole passel o' injuns ridin' around an' cuttin'up.All 'cept one. He was settin' his pony an' starin' like the devil himself. Pizi's hate was plain in his eyes. He spat in my direction, raised his lance to the sky, and screamed the Sioux war cry. He shook his lance at Crazy Horse.

"You are Lakota! You should use the rifle to shoot the white eye dog!" He got real quiet all of a sudden. I could tell that Crazy Horse was getting riled.

"Today, this man will be one of us. He will be a Lakota! We do not kill our brothers!" Pizi knew Crazy Horse didn't take no pushin', so he walked his pony away, still glaring at me. After Pizi left, the hollerin' started again.

"Today was a good day for medicine, and dancing. Today the Lakota had a new warrior. His name was Medicine Horse!"

The next morning, I was all packed and ready to go. Red Cloud put his hand on my shoulder.

"Goodbye, my son. May the Great Spirit guide your steps and mother earth give you shelter."

"Goodbye, Grandfather. My heart is heavy because I must leave my friends, the Lakota. Let us hope for peace between our people."

'Washte! Let us hope! But I do not believe it will happen." Crazy Horse led his pony up beside me.

"I will ride with you now," he grinned. "I wish to talk with you of a most important matter for one last time. I knew this was just an excuse. He was giving me protection Old Red Cloud probably didn't trust some of his braves Contrary to what most white people think, the chief don't have absolute power over his people. If a brave wants to quit in the middle of a fight and go home, he goes right ahead and the chief can't do a thing about it.

We rode out at a walk toward the south and Texas. After ridin' a' ways, somethin' suddenly hit me. I never had found out why Red Cloud had been stompin' around out in that blizzard. I cocked an eye at Crazy Horse. *'Mebbe I could get him to tell me.'*

"There's something I wish to know. What was Grandfather doing out there in the snow? It has been many moons but this I do not understand. Will my friend tell me?"

"Me tell." Crazy Horse answered. 'Grandfather go to sacred mountain. He went to pray to Great Spirit for way to find peace with the White-Eyes. He does not think there is a way but Grandfather goes to make medicine anyway. He leave horse and weapons at foot of mountain. No weapons can go with injun on Sacred Mountain. When Granfather come down, horse gone. Weapons, gone! Blizzard is coming. Grandfather try to walk to village but is long way. No food, no weapons! He grow weak, is cold, him fall in snow. Wolves find, try to kill and eat Grandfather. You chase wolves away."

"You mean his horse got loose?" I squinted at Crazy Horse.

"No get loose. Was taken!" snarled Crazy Horse.

"Crows, huh?" I saw that he was kinda touchy about the subject.

"Not crow! Sioux moccasin tracks! Grandfather see in snow. No say anything. Mebbe catch thief! Him tell everybody, Crows steal horse. We find skeleton of horse and weapons at bottom of canyon."

"But why? Why would one of your people do this thing?" I grimaced faintly. Crazy Horse spat disgustingly

"Grandfather still try to make peace with the White-

Eyes. Some do not want peace! Want war! Grandfather dead, all be for war! Already young braves call for Pizi to lead them against the White-Eyes. Pizi new war chief of Lakota! Him have much power in council. Braves want many scalps, many guns. Braves call for Pizi and one other to lead them upon the Honor Trail. They cry the War Chief's names and dance the war dance!"

"Who is the other war chief?" I watched Crazy Horse with interest. He looked away at the far mountains. I thought for a minute there that he wasn't going to answer me. Then my friend spoke softly.

"Me, Tashunka Witko! Ride fast, friend. Do not look back! Leave the land of the Lakota. From this day forward, there shall be war! You and I must be enemies! If I see you again I will see only an enemy. You must ride with your people as I do. Honor depends that this be so. Ho! Ha! He! Medicine Horse! Ho! Ha! He! My friend!"

Crazy Horse wheeled his horse and raised the Spencer to the sky. He gave the war cry of the Lakota. I felt a shiver hearin' it. There was gonna be a lot of blood on the trail before long. The Bozeman Trail was no place for whites to be, for certain!

'Goodbye Crazy Horse! You are a true friend. I will keep my eyes open! Perhaps I may find you a squaw to warm your blankets! I think that I will have to look far for one so homely as you!" Crazy Horse pranced his horse and grinned. That injun shore loved a good joke! The grin vanished from his face and he spoke soberly.

"It would be wise to keep one's eyes like the hawk. There are those who would take your scalp, my friend. Watch well, for their medicine is strong!" I knew he spoke of Pizi. I watched him gallop away to the North and saw him on a hill sitting the paint war pony which was his favorite. I raised my hand. For answer, he raised the rifle and the Lakota war cry echoed distantly among the mountains. Dropping my head, I felt a deep sadness. I had lost a friend.

"Ho, Ha, He! Crazy Horse! Ride the honor trail!" I said in a whisper. "C'mon you old devil, move it. T'aint safe around here! We gotta' far piece to go an' little time to do it in! Diablo laid back his ears and he snorted. "I know, I know! Ya aint afraid of no injuns, catamounts, bears, boogers, or anythin' that walks on two legs, either! Jest ya' move it, horse, will ya?" Pa's stallion eased into a smooth, ground coverin' lope. I cut to the east and rode a while, hoping to bypass any ambush that might have been set for me. Somehow, I knew it wasn't enough.

At nightfall, there was a shadow to the south west of my line of travel. It looked like an injun. I sighed. Pizi shore didn't let any grass grow under his feet. Pa Rainey's adopted boy was gonna be hard put to keep his hair. I checked the loads in the Winchester. The Russian and my Navy Colt were ready. The Colt rested in my holster and the .44 Russian was tucked down in my waist band handy to my reach. I climbed a hill, working up through the timber to the top, making a cold camp that night and taking out before morning light showed in the east.

No use foolin' myself. I didn't figger I had lost 'em. Somehow I had to come up with something to mess up their party. This was one guest of honor that I didn't mean to show up for the cane raisin'. I thought about what Red Cloud had told me before I left.

"Go far, my son. Do not come back! Already a messenger is come from our cousins, the Cheyenne, telling of a great slaughter at Washita Creek. The blue coats killed all. Few of our people escaped. Soon bluecoats come to

Sioux country. Tribes gather soon in council. Talk is of War with the White-Eyes!"

"Where is this council? Will Red Cloud answer?" I watched the Indian chew on it for a while before he spoke.

"Yes, Is place of plenty grass for many ponies. Injun say, Greasy Grass! White men say, Rosebud! Now you must go from the Lakota. I am your friend, but I am but one among the Lakota. Go! Do not wait for the sun to set upon the mountains! Ho, Ha, He!"

I rode back to the southwest, following a stream that ran fast and swift. I splashed downstream. It was gonna be dark soon. Leaving the water at a place where rock would hide my tracks, I traveled back to the east. Any man that rides a straight line in enemy country has to be a fool.

Making another cold camp that night, I rode steadily all the next day. I wasn't travelling fast and held the horses in. Diablo wanted to run, but I held him back.

"Save your breath, you ol' devil. Yore gonna need it!" I come to a little wooded bluff that was open on all but one side. Fallen trees and brush made a natural breast works on the open side. If Pizi planned to take my scalp, he would have to have a lot of help to do it. If they come across the open, somebody was gonna die. The only way to get to me was to circle and come up through the timber behind me. That would take a long time. It would be well after nightfall, I figured, with a smile.

I looked at the sky. The sun sent crimson streaks among the mountains, and the howl of a wolf made the wilderness seem lonelier than before. After unsaddling and tying the horses, I checked my arsenal. In addition to the two side arms and the Winchester, I still had my Sharps .50. The big gun was deadly at distances up to a thousand yards if handled by the right man. Billy Dixon proved it at Adobe

Wells against Roman Noses' braves. He shot an injun off his horse at just over a thousand yards. Almost a mile! I didn't figure I was as good a shot as Dixon, but I meant to try real hard if'n I was bothered. I never did like to be bothered. Pa Rainey taught me to shoot, and some folks said that Bill Rainey had rode the owl hoot trail. Folks also said that Bill killed the man who murdered his father. Called him out and drilled him dead center with the same Navy Colt that I wore around my waist, fair and square! But it made Bill Rainey an outlaw.

Funny, Pa Rainey was an outlaw but nobody could tell ya just what he had done that was against the law. He rode the backtrails with other hard faced, silent men for five years. Men had died from his fast gun and some had called him a bad man. Then he met Elizabeth Jane. She walked up to him and Bill had met his match. That was the end of Bill's ridin' that trail.

I picketed the horses on the edge of the meadow where the grass was full and green. I had me an idea. I left the horses un-hobbled. If I couldn't outrun Pizi, maybe I could out smart him.

15

~ <u>GOLD!</u> ~

I had me a well fortified position with water and food. I was bankin' on convincing Pizi that I thought I was safe and snug because of Red Cloud's promise. He had promised me safe passage out of the land of his people. If I left the horses in plain sight, it would look like I was off guard and not expectin' anythin'.

A cool spring seeped from granite rock and ran for a small space, disappearing deep underground. I placed my canteens under the small waterfall cascading downward to form a good sized pool. I then built a fire to show that I was real comfortable and settling in. After building the fire, I walked over to fetch the canteens. They were full, and I reached down to take them from the water. A dull glint of metal at the edge of the pool got my attention.

Rushing into the water, I picked up what I thought was a small stone. It was heavy, and blackened with leaf-mold. Upon closer inspection, I nodded my head. Yep! It was gold alright! I stood up holding the nugget in my hand. I looked around real careful but didn't see anything. I knew better though, to play the fool. The birds were singin' and a coyote walked across the meadow. I grinned. Ol' coyote didn't know it, but he'd be my lookout for a while. Dropping down to one knee, I started sifting around, through the black layer of leaf mold at the bottom of the spring. The pool was about four to five feet wide and two feet deep. My first handful yielded only mud and leaf mold. The second was the same. But, the third gave up two more of the pea-sized nuggets. Gold!

Crazy Horse had taken the two small bags of gold dust that I had panned two years before. He had scattered it to the winds and gave my pan to Red Cloud's wife.

"Gold belongs to Indians. Gold bad, bring more White-Eyes to dig in land of Lakota. You are welcome to hunt and fish in owr land. But never try to remove the yellow iron from the waters or the lands of the Sioux! If you do, you shall be our enemy, and we will kill you. The earth is our mother, and we will protect her! Hear well, white man!"

I knew that Crazy Horse meant what he said. My life wouldn't; be worth a plugged nickel if I was caught taking gold! I come up with more nuggets. The spring was full of gold. How? The gold was not round and smooth but rough and jagged. It was mine gold. How had it got to this spot and why in the spring?

I got up and I checked on the coyote. He was still chasing mice in the meadow. I went back to sifting the pool, pulling great handfuls of the sediment from the bottom. From the deepest part of the pool, I took the biggest nugget yet, and the answer to the mystery!

First an old buckle, rusted with a piece of leather still attached. Then with a sucking, slimy sound a rotten pair of old saddle bags came into view. They were real heavy, and my heart gave a jump when I thought about what might be in em. One of the saddle bags was tore with a wide rip.

Both were covered with slime and algae, rotten with their seams coming apart. I carefully pulled the bags over to the ege of the pool, letting the water support the weight. The strap on the whole one came away easily when I pulled and looked inside. There was a whole pile of wet nuggets and small, leather bags. They held gold dust, mor'n likely. It was a massive fortune in gold!

When I was finished, the pool was clean. I searched the ground close by, finding a few more nuggets. Someone had thrown the saddlebags in the pool. The force of the throw had split the bottom of one of the bags, spilling gold in the pool and on the ground all around. I left the bags where they lay and climbed up among the stones above the spring. There among the stones I found a broken gunstock and two pitiful piles of bone. Two skulls lay together at the base of a large boulder. The skulls were broken. *'War Clubs!'*

Among the bones were numerous arrowheads. Truly, the Lakota would protect mother earth, and slay the prospector that wounded her breast! Leaving the bones, I pocketed two belt buckles, one was initialed J.T.

Returning to the pool, I made sure that all signs of what I had done were removed. I threw all the leaf mould back into the pool, along with the empty saddlebags. Leading the horses back and forth through the water made it appear that I had only watered the horses. I put the gold in my own saddle bags, then placed the saddle on Diablo but would ride the buckskin bareback, injun style.

An hour after nightfall, I slipped away after covering the horse's hooves with rawhide. Looking back, the fire was burning brightly. I had left my bedroll, and the packhorse. The animal would move around and make the camp seem occupied. The bedroll I spread next to the fire, filled with rocks. Grinning to myself, I knew. Pizi would be mad as a wet cat. The time loss would be too much to make up if my trick worked, if it didn't I had stacked the odds against me too high to survive. Gripping the Russian in my right hand and walked the horses away slow and easy, I made sure to stay inside the trees to keep from showing myself against the fire. By this time, I would have a guard watching me until the time Pizi chose to attack.

My horse's ears kept pointing over to the left of me and I knew that somewhere there in the darkness, a man waited, watching, to kill me. If I was right, Pizi and his braves were even now slipping up through the timber. But they must be careful, because they knew that my senses had been sharpened by living with them for two years. I was almost as much an Indian as they were. However, they would try to kill me. But I would not be there. With distance there was safety and I intended to be as far away as I could be before morning. Leading the horses, I slipped away into the night! I was headed for Texas and Jori Lee!

The black eyes of Pizi looked down on the white-eye's wagon. Chagrined and frustrated by the escape of his enemy, Pizi would avenge his anger on these two paleface women. They would please his braves very much. The old man with the red hair would die slowly. Pizi would take care of it himself. The war chief looked at Spotted Calf darkly. The brave was the one that Pizi had sent to watch the camp of the single White-Eyes. Spotted Calf claimed that the white-eyes had mounted the Appaloosa and ridden up into the sky on the spotted medicine horse.

'They had flown away like a bird!' Spotted Calf insisted, "And there were no tracks." The wild tale of the brave had delayed the pursuit while the other braves argued about it. Finally, one of the braves discovered tracks far away to the southeast.

"See fool, a horse cannot fly." Pizi had snarled at the brave.

"Does not the bird alight upon the ground again?" Spotted Calf announced smugly. Pizi smoldered with anger. He suspected Spotted Calf of being a spy for Red Cloud. No matter, he had the White-Eyes wagon to take care of at the moment.

"Hopo!" Pizi barked, "We go!" Spotted Calf watched the back of the war chief and amusement shone in his eyes. If he had been a white man, he would have laughed!

Red John knew that something was wrong. His days as a trapper with Bear Claw Chris Lapp, had taught him that. He knew nature's ways. It was too quiet. No coyote, no birds, and even the insects were silent, as if waiting for something to happen. He rode back toward the wagon.

"Miz Rainey, I don't want to frighten' you or the girl, but somethin' is wrong. It could be injuns. Pull up into them trees and we'll fort up for a while. Soon's we git stopped, hobble them mules so's they can't run off with the wagon. Be too slow to run from injuns, anyways. Best way is to fort up and fight em. Make it cost 'em too much. Mebbe they'll give up an' go away if they see it'll cost 'em some."

Libby worked quickly, and Jori Lee jumped down with the guns just as soon as the wagon stopped rolling. The sun was hot, but they had shade and they had water. Red John's eyes searched for a sign of movement.

"Mebbe I'm gittin' jumpy in my old age," John murmered to himself. All was quiet and still, nothing moved. "Guess I made a mistake," he said to himself. "We'll jest set here a spell an' see what happens."

"John." Libby's voice gave him warning. "Up there." Then he saw them. They came slowly, carefully. He counted seven, no, nine, as they walked and slid their horses down a small hill. They stopped and the leader sat his horse silently staring at the wagon. They were Sioux, Ogallallah, bad face Sioux and they were painted for war! Scalps fluttered from the lance-heads, as the wind blew the ponies tails sideways. John leaned forward, holding his breath. The leader was heavy set with a single eagle feather sticking upright from his scalp-lock. The feather was blood-red.

"Hell's fire and tarnation!" John swore vehemently. "That 'un yonder is a Hunkpapa, see him, the leader with the red feather? That's Pizi!" John knew the Indian's reputation. "This is bad, that injun won't give up, no matter if hell freezes over! Git ready, Libby, and you too, Jori Lee. They're gonna come at us now. Hold yore fire 'till I tell ya." The leader of the Indians raised his rifle over his head, and the undulating war cry of the Ogallallah echoed between the hills.

'Hoka Hey, Hopo!" Pizi dropped his arm and the Lakota braves charged. John watched them come.

"Easy now," he bawled, "Now, let 'em have it!" The Winchesters cracked, but not an Indian fell. Red John held his fire. 'I gotta git the chief, else it's the last trail fer us. We won't git another chance!" The big 50 belched fire and smoke.

"Missed, blast it! Libby, Jori Lee, git the leader!" Elizabeth Jane calmly stood up amidst the bullets and aimed her rifle.

"Git down, Ma!" Jori Lee screamed, firing as fast as she could work the leaver of her Winchester.

"Libby!" Roared John, but Libby waited as Pizi galloped closer and closer. Pizi saw her standing, calmly aiming her Winchester at him and he felt contempt for the white squaw's fool heardiness.

"Hokahey!" Pizi raised his rifle to fire, but Libby's rifle cracked first, and Pizi felt a bolt of lightning strike him in the chest. He fell, and rolled over and over into a clump of sage and his body lay still. A wild yell burst from Red John's throat, and he leapt from cover to stand side by side with Libby and their rifle's cracked together. Two braves were tumbled from their ponies to fall heavily on the ground. Then another fell to Libby's Winchester. Jori Lee killed the ponies of two more Indians, and the charge was broken.The stunned braves were picked up by the remainder of the war party as they raced swiftly out of range of the white-eyes guns.

"Libby, you sweet, wonderful woman, you, I could jest kiss ya for that!" Red John gushed.

"Not less'n I say so an' give my permission, you can't!" Libby stated crisply. "Well... I guess it wouldn't hurt nothin'." Red John looked at her with adoration in his eyes, and then kissed her. Jori Lee grinned. It looked like her ma had Red John roped and hogtied, it shore nuff did!

The Sioux braves watched from the hill.

"Hau!" said Hump. "The white man makes love to his woman while we sit here out of range of his guns. It is disgusting!" He spat on the ground.

"Wagh!" Grunted Spotted Calf, "But she is a very fine squaw!" The other braves grinned affirmation. "Wagh!"

"T'aint over yit," Red John warned. "They'll come agin' just as shore as a man is born naked! Oh! Uh... Sorry, Uh, Libby, er Jori Lee! I wasn't watchin' my tongue." Libby and Jori Lee looked at each other and laughed. Suddenly, Red had an idea.

"Libby, Jori Lee, cover me, I'm gonna git the body of their chief. Mebbe we can trade him for safe passage out'a here!" Red John raced for the sage clump that hid Pizi's body.

Libby's bullet had stuck the receiver of Pizi's rifle, glancing upward into the bone breastplate of the chief. It shattered the bone into fragments and cut a shallow groove upwards. Not fatal, but enough to knock Pizi unconscious. However, he was not unconscious now! He lay on his stomach, listening to the footsteps of Red John McDonald grow closer and closer. As the white man grasped his wrist to drag him toward the wagon, Pizi twisted like a cat, jerking Red John backward upon the ground.

"Eeee yaaahhh!" Pizi screamed his war cry, and then plunged his long knife to the hilt into Red John's body! Jori Lee screamed and Libby raised her rifle to fire but she was too late.

"No!" Pizi's knife was blasted from his fingers before he could strike again. Libby stared with surprise as Pizi stood staring at a grove of trees over to her left. She saw him then. A big man rode out from the trees with a pistol in his hand. *'Could it be? Yes, that was Bills appaloosa! Then the man must be…*

"Rance! Oooh Jori Lee, it's Rance!" Elizabeth Jane Rainey began to cry for the first time since her late husband's funeral.

I walked Diablo toward Pizi. The brave held his wrist and stared at me, and then spit at me. The appaloosa snorted and reached swiftly out to bite. Pizi was forced to leap backwards.

"How! Kola, friend!" I smiled, "You are far from your lodge fire! What does my friend Pizi do so far from the lands of the Lakota?" Pizi ignored my question.

"'I am not your friend, White-Eyes!" he growled.

"Pizi's tongue is straight, but his heart is black with

hatred for his enemies. Perhaps this hatred has sickened his head and his heart. Perhaps no more is he a brave warrior or the Great War chief of the Sioux nation! He comes to make war on women while his people gather on the Rosebud. Soon they will fight a great battle against the bluecoats but Pizi is elsewhere riding a trail with no honor! The Lakota fight for their land and their people, but Pizi makes war on squaws! He brings braves with him, braves needed by his people to defend their village!"I was gettin' mad again the more I thought of how he was not there for his people.

"Pizi's heart is bad because of his wife and son who were killed by the bluecoats. I have done nothing against Pizi or his people, yet he desires my blood! My father and mother were killed by the red man, yet I befriended your people! I raised my arms to the braves on the hill.

"Hear me, O' Lakota! I now do that which Pizi had not the honor to do! I challenge him to fight to the death. What does the Lakota say to this?"

The braves looked at one another.

"Aieeee," screamed Spotted Calf, "He is a man! He speaks with honor!"

"No!" Hump growled back. 'He might kill the Lakota!"

"Fool!" argued Spotted Calf, 'He has but to pull the trigger to kill. He speaks as a Lakota! They are both great warriors! It will be a great fight. I would see it! What say you brothers?" The braves howled with approval.

"Ugh! Big Fight!" Spotted Calf raised his hand to the white man.

"It is agreed, my friend. Is it peace, then, my brother?"

"Aieee! It is peace! Washte! We come!" Libby raised her rifle.

"No, don't shoot!" I looked at my adopted ma, "Go

look after Red John, Ma, he's hurt bad! Do what you can for him." Elizabeth threw her rifle down and ran to Red John. She took his head in her lap.

"Oooh, Jori Lee, He's hurt bad! Help me stop the bleeding. Ohhh, John! John!" I dismounted as the Lakota rode up.

"How! Kola, Medicine Horse!" grinned Spotted Calf.

"Rance! Are these savages your friends?" Jori cried out.

"I lived with them for two years, Jori, they are fighting men, but they are no more savages than the men who steal their land and murder their children. C'mon, let's get John in the wagon." I grasped him under the shoulders, Libby and Jori Lee each took a leg. Even so, we had to go slow an' easy.

"There," Libby said. "Now, heat me up some water, Jori Lee." Libby hovered over Red John like a mother hen. "It's bad, Rance, I can't seem to stop the bleeding." I looked at John's face. It was pale and blue-lookin'. Spotted Calf sauntered up beside me.

"Him die soon, you no give medicine!" I perked my ears up. I had learned to pay attention to every word these injuns said.

"What kinda' medicine?" I hoped that it was real medicine, and not any of that whoopin' an' hollerin' some of the medicine men did.

"Poultice! Me make poultice. Come, you help!"

"Pizi may not want to wait." I said

"Him wait. Him accept challenge to fight. No run off. Loose face with braves. Him wait, you betcha! Now we save old Red Beard!" I couldn't believe my ears. This same injun had once calmly disemboweled a captive right in front of my eyes. Now, he was gonna doctor a white man! Nobody could figger what an injun would do. We set to work, quick!

Red John was dreaming. He dreamed of being scalped by a war painted injun. Then another injun put smelly poultices on the wound. A Sioux doctorin' a white man?

"Awww John, yore a goner for shore! Yore outta yore head! Libby, Libbby, honey, I love you but I'm a goner!" Red John didn't know it but he was talking out loud and Elizabeth Rainey heard him. She cried out,

"Oh John! You're alright! You talked! Talk to me, John! Darlin'!"

"Ah c'aint," mumbled Red John. "Ah'm daid!"

"Ohhh, John, open your eyes, you're not dead! You are going to be alright!" John opened one eye.

"Ah h'aint, daid? I mean?

"No, open your eyes, John." He opened up both eyes then.

"Ha! Guess ah h'aint, at that! Where we at? An' what am I doin' naked under this blanket? Libby!" He pulled the blanket up to his chin modestly.

"You were wounded, John. You were out of your head for a while. You kept yellin' Kid! Rainey! There's another un!"

"Well," he grumbled. "That kid was the best friend thet this child ever had! Saved my life once, and him being yore son don't hurt none, either."

"Adopted son," corrected Libby. "And he's right outside the wagon. He saved your life again, John."

"What!" The kid? Where's he at? Lemme see!" John tried to get up, but Libby pushed him back down.

"No, John, You'll start the bleeding again. Now, I want to know if you remember what you said just now? Do you, John?" Libby asked sweetly.

"What ye mean?" John didn't like the look in her eye.

He'd seen that look before, it usually got some pore feller in a heap o' trouble. Marryin' trouble! He looked away.

"You spoke a while ago, John. You called me honey. An' you said you loved me. Is it true, John? Do you love me?" She leaned closer and closer, smiling like an angel. John dropped his eyes. There was a lump as big as Texas in his throat He swallowed hard.

"Ah reckon so, hon- er.. Libby." He choked.

'Ohhhh! John! Darlin!" Libby kissed Red on the mouth, again and again.

Me and Jori Lee was grinning at each other. We knowed what was happenin' Finally, I poked my head under the canvas.

"Hi, old timer! You ain't makin a pass at my ma, now, are ya?" I had to duck before a red-faced, splutterin, mountain man kicked me in the face. Instead he hit the oak tail gate of the wagon with his bare foot!

"Owww! Dad burn that kid! He broke muh foot! You jest wait, you dad blamed, runny-nosed brat, I'm gonna....!

"John!" Libby scolded! "Such language! An' in front of a lady, too!"

"Oh! Sorrry!" John apologized. Libby climbed down out of the wagon bumping her head on the iron hoop.

"Dang it!" she gritted.

"Huh? What was that?" John asked.

"Nothin' John, darlin, go on back to sleep now."

"Don't wanna, Ah wanna talk to tha kid. Hey kid, c'mere!"

"No! John." Libby's face puckered up like she was ready to cry.

"What's the matter?" John looked at her. "What's wrong? Woman, say somethin'!"

"He's challenged that chief to a fight! Oh, John, what

if?" Libby couldn't hold her tears any longer. She leaned her head on the tailgate of the wagon.

"What? No! The kid fight Pizi? Plumb suicide! That injun's a murderer! Killed a heap o' men! No! Don't let him do it!

"I'm afraid that there's nothin' that we can do, John, nothin' but pray!" Libby looked at Jori Lee, whose face showed a white, strained expression. Her eyes followed the tall, lean man in the buckskins.

I walked up to where Spotted Calf sat playin' the bone game with his friends. He looked up.

"You fight now?" Spotted Elk exclaimed excitedly, leaping up from the ground.

"Yes, we fight now!" I looked at Pizi with serious hardened eyes.

16
~ THE CHALLENGE ~

"Washte," Pizi said! "Me kill you quick!" The Indian glared at me. I spoke softly,

"I reckon yore honor wouldn't let ya back down, now, would it? Seein' as how you're War Chief an' all?"

"No!" Pizi growled, and he drew himself up to his full height.

"I thought so!" I said. I didn't like Pizi no better than he did me. It was about time that we got things settled between us for good!

"Washte," Spotted Calf grinned! "It will be a great fight! Me bet all on fight. Hah! Me win much, you betcha! Me be rich injun!"

"Waah!" Hump looked disgusted. "First we fight, then we friends, now we fight again! This crazy war party! Me stay in teepee next time!" Pizi picked knives just like I knew he would. The ornery redskin was good with a knife. Guns, now, I'd shade him and he knew it. Spotted Calf drew a big circle in the dirt, then all the Indians took up positions around the circle. If either of us got outside the circle, we were fair game for the lancers. I knew the game. The object was as much to throw your opponent out of the circle as it was to knife him and anything else to win. They wasn't any rules.

Two razor sharp knives were stuck in the ground in the center of the circle. Whoever, got to 'em first, had the other man at his mercy. An' I knew better than to expect any mercy from Pizi! Hump was ready to give the signal.

I had taken off my guns and handed them to Spotted Calf. Just as I turned, Humps arm dropped, catchin' me off guard. I threw myself forward but it was just too late. Pizi moved like a mountain lion. He got to the knives first and kicked the last one out of the circle! I was unarmed!

I had to scramble back quick! Pizi crouched, his eyes full of hate. Then he slid forward.

"Now, White-Eyes die!" I had just one chance. I dropped my head and stood still, jest like I was givin' up. I gave a real big sigh and said in the Sioux dialect,

"Hokahey, So let it!" Pizi's eyes showed his satisfaction. He moved forward and thrust for the jugular vein in my throat. At the last second, I shifted, taking the knife in my shoulder. The blade burned as it went deep into my flesh. Then I hit Pizi in the face with my fist. I smashed his nose and lips with the blow. I grabbed his knife arm before he could recover, and drove my knees into his belly. The air whooshed out of him, and he sat down on the ground.

I pulled the knife out of my shoulder. Raising it for all to see, I cut a lock of hair from Pizi's head and held it up! "Haieeee! I claim it! H'gun! H'gun!" The braves echoed my coup! It was one of the most respected of deeds to the Indians. My enemy was alive and still dangerous. Pizi got to his feet and his face was ugly. I had shamed him. I held the knife before me as he charged.

"Me kill White-Eyes!" he screamed. He was wild with

rage. I didn't want to kill an unarmed man. I tried to sidestep, but the injun slammed into my bleeding shoulder and I gasped with pain. The force of Pizi's charge carried me to the ground. I rolled away, realizing that I could still lose if I didn't kill him. But I just couldn't.

Stepping backward, I drove the knife into the ground. All of a sudden I got mad, real mad! I guess I was half mad at myself for being such a fool! I turned to Pizi.

"There is your weapon, Pizi! Come and get it!" I watched him come and I hit him in the nose again, breaking it and spattering blood. He staggered backwards

Come," I smiled coldly. "Take your weapon!" Pizi looked at me with watering eyes. He slid forward, faining at that last moment, trying to dive past me for the knife! He almost made it. I kicked him in the head. He rolled over, almost rolling outside the circle. Scrambling, he tried to avoid the lance of the braves on that side. He made it.

He stared at me out of eyes that were swelling fast. *Both his eyes would soon be blackened and swollen shut,'* I thought just as a wave of dizziness wafted over me. I had made a mistake. I forgot about the blood I was losin'! The dizziness passed, but Pizi had realized my weakness. He grinned evilly. Folding his arms, he waited. The loss of blood would defeat the white man.

'I better do somethin' Pa,' I said to myself. I clutched at my shoulder and staggered. Pizi thought his time had come. He leaped forward! Somebody ought to have told him about playin' possum. I hit him real fast, my fist thudded' into his face. I punched him in the eyes, and then hard into his stomach, doubling him up! As he hunched over, I gave it to him hard and vicious in the kidneys. He fell to the ground. When he tried to git up, I brought my knee up into this face, busting his lips!

"That's fer Yo'wesa!" I glared, and then I picked up the knife. Pizi was out cold on the ground. I walked from the circle.

"You no kill?" Spotted Calf asked, surprised.

"No! I claim his life!" This was the greatest of shames to the Indians. "Take him from my sight!"

'So be it!" Spotted Calf grunted. 'Make travois!" he told the Lakota braves. "We go to Rosebud!" He turned back to me. "Washte, me rich now. Win all horses! Hah! Them much mad! Feel bad!" Spotted Calf pointed at Hump and his brothers. I eyed Hump. I hadn't liked the way he had jumped the gun with his signal. He had done it deliberately, I figgered. Spotted Calf spoke again, low.

"The next time you leave camp in enemy country, Medicine Horse, do not ride under such large tree." I looked at him, realizing that this man was the one back at the camp by the spring. He could have killed me easily. I even remembered the tree. "The grandfather looks after his son's, my brother. Ho! Ha! He! Go in peace, Medicine Horse!" He waved his arm to the Northwest. "Hopo! Let's go!"

I watched as the braves galloped away. Pizi was sure getting a rough ride. It was clear that he had lost face with the braves. The travois bounced and skidded across the ground wildly.

After getting Libby and Red John comfortable in the wagon and Diablo tied to the back of it, I climbed up in the seat beside Jori Lee. I wound the long, leather, wagon reins around my hand while I looked at her and grinned. She grinned back, and then leaped into my arms to kiss me. Pulling away, she said

"What if they run away?" I looked at the mules.

"They wouldn't dare at a time like this!" I scowled. Jori

Lee laughed and came back into my arms. It felt wonderful to have my Jori Lee back! I had missed the scent of her hair and the color of the blue sky in her eyes. I missed the way her pink lips softly framed her teeth, all moist when she smiled in the sun.I sat and took the sight of her sitting there beside me like someone who had been dying of thirst, drinking her in while my heart was leaping in my chest. She must have understood how I felt because she seemed to be doing the very same thing.

Jori Lee looked at her man. He was big, strong and handsome. He had grown and she felt a safe feeling being with him where it had not been before. There was also wildness in him that she knew she would not be able to tame. Even so, it felt right. It caused a desire for him inside of her that was new and wonderful. No woman could ever be satisfied with a coward.

This was a time of freedom and lawlessness. The law would soon be out in this territory, she worried. Rainey had a price on his head. She's showed Rance the handbill.

"Oh, what'll we do?" she asked him tearfully.

"Whatever, it takes to clear my name, honey," he said. "I got to. I can't ask you to marry me as long as I'm running from the law. But, there ain't gonna be no more runnin'! Red Cloud made me see that the best way is to fight. I got to be a man, or else I don't deserve you or those two wonderful friends back there in the wagon. A man's gotta have honor, or else he don't amount to nuthin'!"

Jori Lee hugged him fearfully.

"We'll be in Dodge soon I mumbled. "It's a Rough town full of rough men. You stick close to me, Jori Lee. I reckon Red John will be alright as long as Libby's around to protect him." We both laughed.

In Dodge City, Kansas, the men in dusty trail-worn

clothes sat at a plank table nailed to a barrel. Buck Dexter glared at the sherrif,

"Cousin, seems like ye've brought us on a wild goose chase. We hain't seen neither hide nor hair o'them females nor that red headed old man fer three weeks now. An' hit's been two weeks since we met anybody that has seen 'em! I'm getting mighty put out over it!" Buck's eyes pinned the little man to his chair.

"Now don't ye fret none, cousin, they're out there, they gotta be! Hain't their trail been straight as an arrer' this way? Jest keep yore shirt on, an we'll make a pile o' greenbacks! That old man will have to bring 'em females into Dodge sometime. H'it's the only civilized place this side of injun country!"

"Thet's just it! Th' injuns could'a got 'em!" Buck rose up in his chair and his yellow eyes got mean-lookin'. "If'n ye brought us way out h'yar fer nuthin'....."

'N-N- Now, cousin, don't go getting' all upset, we'll git 'em, ye just wait an' see! I kin feel it in ma bones!

"Yeh,"Buck drawled 'If'n we don't git em, that's just what ye'll be, bones!" The sheriff swallowed hard, and then tossed his drink down. It burned his throat and he wheezed.

"Hain't they no decent likker in this town?" The batwings burst open and Jase Dexter rushed over to the table, his spindly legs swinging.

'They're hyar!" he announced, pleased with himself. "They're down at the mercantile buyin' grub. An' they're payin' with gold! I jest seen 'em! The kid's with em, too. He's the one's thet's got the gold! Want I should take him? Jase patted his forty four.

"Well, well, well!" Buck drawled, scrubbing his black beard, then he got to his feet. "Who'd a thought it?"

"I tol' ja!" The sheriff said gleefully. "An' gold, fer the takin, too! Hee hee!

"Let's go!" Buck stomped toward the batwings followed by the snickering Jase. Sheriff Dexter brought up the rear.

Me an' Jori Lee stepped out on the boardwalk. We had our arms full of brown paper wrapped packages.

"Oh, Rance, it's jest wonderful!" Jori's eyes sparkled. "We're together again an' you have enough gold fer us to live on fer the rest of our lives! All my dreams have come true! Oh, I'm so happy thet my heart could jest explode!"

"Me too, Jori Lee," I grinned. "I jest wish Pa was here to see it." I missed Pa so much it hurt thinking about what he would say. Jori Lee said,

"Pa's in heaven, jest as happy as us. I loved him but I also love Red John, too. Now, if you'd just ask me to-. ..." The plate glass window beside us shattered as bullets sang all around us, thudding into the plank walls. The owner of the store jumped down behind the counter.

"Git down, Jori Lee!" I shoved her behind the wagon, takin' a bullet in the left leg. It buckled under me and I fell in the dust of the street. I saw a man walking toward me firing his gun. One of his slugs jerked my hat off my head. Another tugged at my sleeve but by that time I had shot him in the chest. He staggered, and then he kept comin' He was a big man with a black beard. I had seen him before! Lifting my Russian, I shot him again, twice in the face. He fell heavy.

More shots sent dust into my eyes. I couldn't see! I fired at a running shape that dodged an' twisted across the street. Once, then twice I had missed. My last shot brought the man down. Rubbing my eyes, I saw that he was gettin' up. I had only winged him! Again, I wiped my eyes and was gritting my teeth, still half-blinded from the dirt spray. My

Russian clicked empty and I reached for the Navy.
Somehow the thong holding it in my holster got broke and
the gun lay ten feet away by the hitch rail. That thin, skinny
man staggered toward me, holdin' his guts in with his hand.
I noticed that he was laughing crazy-like.

"Make yore peace to the Lord above, Kid, an' thanks fer
uppin' my cut of that reward money!" He cackled.
Something big hit him in the chest and he was throwed
backwards a full summersault, landing on his face. I turned
my head to see who had fired. Elizabeth Jane Rainey come
slowly crawlin' up over the wagon's tailgate, shaking and
holding her head. She was clutching the big fifty caliber
rifle that belonged to Red John and the barrel was still
smoking!

"Ohhh..! It went off a'fore I wuz ready!" she mumbled.
Her right eye was slowly turning black. Jori Lee broke out
from under the wagon, rushing over to me.

"Rance! Yore hurt!" She was cryin' while she tore up her
petticoat. Then tearin' up my pants leg to get to the wound
she winced as the damage to my leg was ugly. She then
wrapped the wound tightly. I heard the zing of another
bullet as it tore through her full skirts. It ricosheted from
the board walk and broke the other plate glass window of
the store. Another bullet fanned my cheek, as I dove to
retrieve my Navy. Libby came back up over the tailgate of
the wagon with her Winchester ready. Her eye was
completely black and blue, now. I could hear Red John
roaring with indignation and asking what was going on.

I raised my Navy pistol as a small, runt of a man was
shoved out into the street from the alley which was across
from the wagon.

"N-N-Now, hold on thar, I'm an officer of the law, too!
I come with my deppities to 'rest this feller! He's wanted

fer murder down in Texas! An' th' rest of 'em are 'complices! Ow! Quit yore shovin'! I tol' ja, I'm a sheriff!" Three men were helping Dexter across the street none too gently.

"Git along there, back-shooter!" The one with the bowler held a colt in his hand. Jori Lee started bandaging me again. She took on over me terrible!

"Ya alright, son?" The man kneeled at my side. He had a mustache.

"Yeah, I guess I'll be alright." I grunted. I noticed the Marshall's badge on his vest. The Marshall's eyes were blue and he looked at me real steady-like. I'm the town Marshall, son, and this here is U.S. Marshall, Jacob March. I reckon ya know 'tother un!"

"Johnny? Johnny Hansen, you ol' son of a gun!"

"Hello Rance!" Johnny grinned. "Marshall here has got somethin' to tell ya." The man called Jacob March stepped up and his badge looked as big as a house to me.

"You Rance Rainey?" he asked gruffly. I swallowed hard. Well, here it comes….

"Yeah!" I finally got out.

"Yer under arrest fer murder!" Jori Lee jumped up,

"No! It was self defense! I seen the whole thing! You can't arrest him! The Marshall grinned.

"No matter, I got a pardon for him from the new governor o' Texas. Yore young friend here who is now an' aspirin' lawyer, took yore case to the new governor right after election. You've been found innocent of thet murder charge! I reckon ya owe him a' plenty!"

"Ohhh, Johnny!" Jori Lee hugged the young man, and kissed him.

"Thanks Johnny," I blurted, gratefully.

"Now, hold on h'yar," Dexter blustered. "This man's

my prisoner. Don't I git th' reward fer capturin' him? I know a lotta 'portant people an…" The U.S. Marshall glared.

"No! Yah ain't, back shooter! An' yore under arrest fer murder, attempted murder, rustling, and mebbe a few more lil' things jest as soon as thet wire gits back from Missouri! Yore pal Swain, is in jail fer rustlin' and swindlin', an' he's talkin' his fool head off. Cattlemen's association hired us to trace them cattle ya took. Green hides tell the story. The governor sent me to collect you an' yore friends, an' bring this kid his pardon! Now, git on over to the jail! Pronto!" The man with the bowler hat tipped it to the women folks.

"Names Bat Masterson, ladies. Welcome to Dodge City Anythin' I can do for ya', just let me know." He looked at me.

"Good luck, son!" He turned to follow Dexter and the U.S. Marshall. But he stopped, and turned.

"By the way, Mrs. Rainey, the deed to your ranch is waitin' fer ya back in Texas. An' damages fer yore stock will be paid by the bank." He touched his hat.

"Thanks a' heap Marshall." Libby was overcome with gratitude. "Blessed man!" Masterson smiled, and then he was gone. Ma's eye looked funny. I laughed.

"What are you laughin' at, young man?" Libby huffed. "Hain't ya never seen no black eye before?" Jori giggled. "Well I never!" Libby put her hands on her hips.

"Oh! Rance, yore free!" Jori Lee grabbed me and cried for joy.

"Will somebody git me out of hyar an' tell me what th' heck's goin' on?" Bellowed Red John.

"Yes, John," Libby said sweetly, takin' her own sweet time about it.

"S'bout dad burn time!" John grumbled.

I sat there in the dust of the street and thought about Red Cloud and Crazy Horse. I thought of the Lakota people. They fought for their homes and their people. Somehow in my minds eye I could see a great battle. I could hear bugles sounding retreat, and war cries echoed deep in my mind.

"Hokahey, hopo! Let's go! It's a good day to die!" They were fighting men, and they rode the honor trail. I thought also of Yo'wesa. The sweet sparrow that I had for only a short time was flying through the heavens above telling how her husband was a great warrior.

Looking at Jori Lee Rainey, standin' there with her hands on her hips, I could see her foot tappin' angrily.

"Well Rance Rainey, are ya gonna ask me to marry ya or not?" Her eyes flashed and I decided right then, *'it was not a good idea to mention Yo'wesa.'* There were some things a man jest had to keep quiet about, honor or no honor!

"Shore, darlin, lets go find us a preacher!"

"John," Libby asked sweetly.

"Well." John grumbled, "Ah reckon we might as well make it a' double weddin'! C'mon Libby." Red John said.

"Yes, John," she answered, takin' him in her arms. They staggered off down the street. Me an' Red John was limpin' and grinnin' at each other.

"Shore, Christmas, ain't it jest like old times?" Red John whooped a big Texan, "Yeeeeeh haaaaaw!"

~ *The End* ~

~~~

Leopard Appaloossa

Diablo, Devil Horse

(Un-Kah-Gah Shoon-kah ker)

~~~

~ ABOUT THE AUTHOR ~

Jim Wade Smith, was born and raised in the Appalachian, mountains of North Carolina. Growing up under Mount Mitchell and near Grandfather Mountain, the family was poor and lived in a shack built of sawmill planks.

A Diphtheria survivor, at the age of four, he miraculously survived the old country doctor's, "Kill or Cure shot." This was actual words that the doctor used for the description of the medicine that he administered. At the time there was no cure for the illness and the medicine was a long shot whether it would help him recover.

He played minor league baseball so well that he garnered a contract offer for the Brooklyn Dodgers but being only 19, he was too young to sign the contract His father refused to sign, stating,

"I need you here, boy." His father was illiterate and could not read the contract himself.

Jim has written occasionally over his life time. This western novel, Rance Rainey was originally written in the 80's, and entered into a Louis L'amour book competition under the name "Honor Trail." It placed second but Jim had not been able to publish it until now.

At the young age of 74, Jim is a retired brick mason and still is a dead eye deer hunter. You can find him studying his King James Bible, writing his mountain short stories and excerpts. His other novel, "Call of the Dove," was just recently published and its sequel is soon to be released

An ordained minister, married to his wife, Trina McKinney Smith, of over 50 years, Jim is a grandfather and now a great granddad! Someone once asked him what did he pray for the most? With tear-filled, gentle eyes he answered,

"the little children of the world!"

~ *Jim Wade Smith* ~

~~~

www.ingramcontent.com/pod-product-compliance
Lightning Source LLC
Chambersburg PA
CBHW050524260626
47157CB00004B/1454

* 9 7 8 0 6 9 2 7 3 1 2 6 0 *